D1738447

THE EBOLA GAME

A Dr. Scott James Thriller

GLENN SHEPARD

MYSTERY HOUSE

www.glennshepardauthor.com

Mystery House Publishing, Inc.

Newport News, VA

ISBN 0-9971349-1-7

ISBN 978-0-9971349-1-9

Cover and interior design by Annie Biggs and Scott Line

Printed in the United States of America.

THE EBOLA GAME

Chapter 1

Day 1
The Hospital Administrator's Office
Jackson City Hospital
10:00 a.m.

 "WE HAVE TO GET some of these cadavers processed," he said.

"Hey, I just work here."

"Scott, I'm serious. I need some help with this stuff. I need you to call down to the county coroner's office and get those people moving. Our refrigerator is full and they say they're too backed up to get to us."

Talking to Ray, the Facilities Manager of my hospital, was always hell.

"And I'm going to have to hire an outside plumber," he went on, "We're all backed up in Gastroenterology."

"You mean the *toilets* ... are backed up, Ray."

"That's affirmative. Have a nice day, Dr. James."

Another day as the Chief Administrator of The Jackson City Hospital. I run this place because I'm a scapegoat, an outcast. This is the "community hospital," which means we take a lot of patients that nobody wants. It also means that sometimes there's no one to claim the dead. It also means that sometimes our plumbing isn't perfect.

I didn't mind running the hospital. It was a cause I always believed in. I'd been doing charity work ever since I became a doctor and I liked it. I'm a craniofacial surgeon. I fix people's faces.

Or, I used to.

After the phone conference with the facilities manager, I sat back in my chair. Mary Wiggins, my assistant, hearing me get off of the phone, strolled in to say, "Allen Sarverman called about twenty minutes ago. He said he has a letter that says the North Carolina Board of Medicine has restored the license of a Dr. Scott James, to practice medicine and surgery, without restrictions."

"You're kidding."

She looked at me with a frown. "Do you know this guy, Dr. Scott James?"

I jumped out of my chair and hugged her. I couldn't help it. I couldn't believe it. This was a profound moment for a person like me.

You could call me a target. I guess that's better than "pariah." My life has played out in the headlines over the past two years but you wouldn't know it. I live a semi-submerged, semi-protected, semi-guilty, always-under-observation lifestyle. So I have no freedom. I am a person, according to what little I know about my "file," who is "known to be in association with ... " and "loosely connected to ..."

That's me.

"Allen said he just got the letter and he closed down his law office for the day and canceled his appointments, and he doesn't care if people are upset. He's coming over with a couple of bottles of champagne. But he says he doesn't know what *you're* going to drink."

I had to laugh at that. "Thank God for my lawyer."

The blast of an ambulance siren pierced the air and I turned away from Mary to look out my window at the ER. This was a common occurrence at a Level One Trauma Center, happening ten-to-twenty times a day, but I always wanted to see the exciting and never-duplicated scene of the doctors and nurses rushing out to meet the ambulances.

The emergency vehicle was pulling in, and, thankfully, so was the black Lexus of Allen Sarverman. "There's Allen," I said, as the car disappeared into the parking garage next to the ER. And then there was a blinding white flash.

A deafening *BOOM* exploded from the ER and then the drywall on one side of my office disintegrated in front of me, and I was suddenly on my side with my head turned up and the ceiling collapsing. The white cloud of plaster all around me lit up, brilliantly, and then I realized that sunlight was flooding the room. A white cloud of plaster dust. An acrid smell of sulfur. A scream from Mary right as the blast hit, but now eerie silence. A feeling of numbness all over my body.

I shivered for a moment, then started wiping the dust from my eyes and looking around the room. There was an arm sticking from the broken plaster where Mary had stood. The white dust was everywhere, choking me and getting in my eyes. I stood, slowly, while dust fell from every part of my body and clothing. I started clawing at the debris where Mary had been standing. I strained to lift a joist with a hunk of wall attached to it and then I saw her underneath. Her blue blouse was saturated with blood. The falling joist had crushed her chest. I knelt down and wiped away plaster from her face. Her breathing was shallow, and then I saw her take her last breath. Tears filled my eyes. I lifted her head and softly kissed her hair.

Wiping the tears and the dust away from my face, I realized that the door to my office had been blown into the hallway. I ran out and started down the half-collapsed stairway, heading for the Emergency Room.

What I saw when I got there was incredible. I stood in an open space. I looked up toward what had once been the ceiling and saw only bright sunlight. The ambulance was not there. In the place where I'd last seen it was a huge blast zone, thirty feet in diameter.

<u>Chapter 2</u>

Dr. Scott James' Home
10:00 a.m.

JACQUES JACOBO, "JAKJAK" TO his friends, sat in the darkness of the living room, looking out from behind the curtains, watching a black SUV drive by the house. Being a bodyguard all those years had given him the habit of constant vigil. He'd sensed something, and as usual his instincts were right. The SUV came rolling by again. That was twice in the past ten minutes.

The street, the house, even the United States, were all very new for Jakjak. With the exception of two brief trips to France, guarding government officials, he'd rarely left his native Haiti. Though he was practicing, his English was still very rough. He spoke with a heavy French accent and with the lilting inflection of his Haitian patois.

Jakjak was thirty-nine, built like a champion athlete, and, thanks to Dr. James, he would be starting classes in the fall to become an X-ray technician. No more Haiti for a while. No more guarding people that other people want to assassinate.

The home in Jackson City and life in the US mixed strangely with his background. He alternated between feeling safe and feeling like he was part of a dangerous game. Being friends with Scott James and living in the doctor's house frequently made him feel like he was living in an armed camp.

Elizabeth Keyes, Scott James' girlfriend, came into the front room with her luxurious hair piled up over her head, looking like she was going some place high-priced, although Jakjak knew that she was going nowhere. She was a virtual prisoner in the house, at least for the time being.

Elizabeth Keyes' term as an informant, an "asset," was coming to an end. She'd given them all they needed, told them all they wanted to hear. Things were easing up. No more running for her life, she thought. No more Omar Farok. Things were going pretty well with her and Scott James. Maybe I should become a consultant, she thought, get a hairdo and an attitude and go on CNN. They have those well-dressed-types on TV all the time, billed as Ex-Intelligence Operatives. I know more than those chicks do, and I can look good, too. And I'm a *real* spy, Honey. Now that it was all winding down, maybe high-dollar "consulting" was the way to go.

"What are you looking at?" she asked.

Jakjak, in his evolving brand of English, said, "De ees a blak ess-u-vee out de."

Keyes peered out from behind the closed curtains. The SUV was driving by again. "Uh oh," she said. "What the hell is going on with the cops?"

She could see the police car that always guarded the house and she could see at least one guy in it, but why wasn't he doing anything?

"I think they've gone to sleep, or at least one of them has."

The pistol she kept on her was Scott James' expensive Browning. The size of the big weapon in its holster was the reason her wardrobe had recently expanded to include a couple of loose-fitting but fashionable jackets.

Keyes chambered a shell and Jakjak instinctively reached into his own jacket and rested his hand on his holster.

The door of the SUV opened and a man dressed in black ran at a crouch toward the house. For some reason the driver just sat there, looking around but not attacking.

Jakjak and Keyes watched the man run across the yard toward the front door of the house. They heard the screen door creak as it opened, both took aim, anticipating that it would be breached, and then the screen door slammed shut. Stunned, Keyes and Jakjak looked out the window to see the man running back to the SUV.

Keyes bolted from the window to the door. She seemed to be on a mission, Jakjak thought. She yanked the door open, burst through the screen, raised the Browning, and took aim at the runner as he was reaching the SUV. She didn't have the shot. She took off running. Jakjak, now on the porch, wondered what Keyes was going to do next.

As the SUV started to pull away, Keyes ran into the street and stopped in front of the hulking vehicle. The SUV lurched, tires squealing. It happened so fast that Keyes hesitated for a split second, and then it was too late. She pointed the Browning at the SUV for an instant, and then flung herself to the side. The black SUV skimmed by her body and then she heard the loud *thump* of the vehicle's fender glancing off the parked car behind her. She heard the roar of the engine, gaining strength, and then disappearing.

Keyes sat up and wiped the sweat from her brow and took a deep breath. Doors began to open, up and down the street. Faces looked out from windows. Everybody already knew that there was "something going on at that house."

Keyes stood and quickly tucked her gun under her jacket and began to run toward the patrol car.

The driver, sitting upright, was still, with his head slumped down at an angle. She spoke, then shook his shoulder. He fell to the side, on top of the body of the second cop. Blood oozed from the backs of both of their heads.

She felt herself trembling as she hurriedly walked back to the house.

Jakjak was still at the front steps, but he was sweating. Behind him hung an ordinary piece of paper, taped to the door, with a message, scrawled in purple magic marker, written by the hand of someone deeply disturbed:

DR. JAMES, YOU ARE BUT A PAWN IN MY EBOLA GAME. DEAREST ELIZABETH IS MY QUEEN. ARE YOU READY TO PLAY?

It was not signed. There was no need to sign it.

Omar Farok.

The unmistakable *pock* of a distant concussion broke the air in the direction of The Jackson City Hospital. Keyes turned and looked in the direction of the explosion. "Jakjak, watch the kids. Watch the boys."

"Nothin weel happon to de boys. Ova my ded body."

Keyes pushed past Jakjak and into the house. As she came out, car keys in hand, she said, "I'm going to the hospital."

"Good luck, Mademoiselle."

Chapter 3

Jackson City Hospital
10:15 a.m.

THE CAR CAME ROARING up and screeched to a halt in front
of the blast zone. It was Keyes. She jumped out, dodged
the debris, and ran to me. She nearly knocked me over as
she jumped into my arms. "You're okay?"

I instinctively cringed. It was the first time I had seen
Elizabeth out in the open and without any protection in
almost a year. When she was *even out*. She only seemed
to go between locked doors and she was always with
somebody. Seeing her out seemed to scream of danger.

I looked at her in amazement. "What are you doing
here?"

"There was somebody at the house. Farok's men. They killed the two cops and then—"

"Are Scotty and Jeremy okay—"

"They're fine. Jakjak's with them. Nobody's getting through him to your boys."

Keyes and I began to dig into the rubble. The devastation was incredible. The police and fire pulled up one at a time and soon it was a swarm. Hospital employees streamed from their jobs to stand, open-mouthed, and look. Cars from the street stopped and their occupants gawked. The sounds of sirens in the distance, coming toward the hospital, were all around us. Suddenly Elizabeth shouted, "Here's someone!"

I ran to her side to find a bloody man covered in plaster dust. I wiped his face, but the lifeless form was not one of my employees. Then I saw three people in a pile, or parts of them. Keyes and I dug all around to find the mangled bodies of two men and a woman, all African-looking, and dressed in black cotton jump suits. None worked for the hospital.

"The ambulance must have been bringing these people here," I said. "What are these people supposed to be, migrant farm workers?"

Their clothing was very simple, strangely so.

Keyes began to cry softly. "This can only be the work of one entity. Farok did this. He'll chase us until we're both dead. He's going to get us this time, Scott. We're never going to be free of this."

My only feeling was to sort out the casualties. I thought of going to the operating room to do what I loved best: operate. But that was not my mission now. I was the hospital administrator, a job much bigger than that of a surgeon who singles out a survivor and operates to save an individual life. I had to direct the entire recovery operation, which, in a 250 bed hospital, involved over a thousand people.

I placed a call to the hospital operator, who, thankfully, was still functioning. "This is Dr. James. Activate the Emergency Response Protocol. Call all physicians in all specialties and tell them to meet me in the hospital lobby. And notify the OR. Have them prepare as many operating rooms as they can. Do that right now, and then call in all personnel from all shifts. We need everybody."

Hospital Lobby
10:25 a.m.

THERE WAS A STEADY stream of walking wounded coming into the lobby. Most were the injured from the second floor, by my administrator's office. I doubted that there would be many survivors from the ER.

The responding group of doctors and nurses were gathering in the lobby, as well. Half a dozen surgeons, family practitioners, and internists were there.

Keyes took me aside to wipe the blood and grime from my face and arms. I was still processing what she'd been telling me about her morning at the house. "If Omar wanted you dead," I whispered to Keyes, "why would his men run away from you? They could have taken you hostage and driven away."

She shrugged and whispered, "I don't know."

Over a hundred people were congregating, awaiting my direction. John Lovit, the only surviving ER physician from the morning shift, was assigned to be in charge of triage. He'd already called in the eight evening and night shift docs to help. I assigned another dozen family docs, internists, and pediatricians to look after the walking wounded.

I was improvising all the way. Thankfully, Edward Huggins, the current Chief of Surgery, hadn't been near the blast. After a quick talk, he went back to direct the operating rooms. We needed general and thoracic surgeons, neurosurgeons, and orthopedists in the main operating rooms. I directed all other surgeons to float between surgery, triage, and the "New ER." This, we decided, could best be set-up in the outpatient surgery center, adjacent to the main operating rooms. Here, we set up minor operating beds, and doctors who hadn't put a stitch in a patient for years were suddenly sewing up minor cuts.

I put the laboratory staff on 24/7 duty until further notice and got the lab technicians churning x-rays from every machine in the hospital, turning out hundreds of pictures of bones.

I told the police to cordon-off the hospital from visitors and rid us of the well-intending outsiders who were already getting in the way, then directed all the maintenance workers and nursing assistants to dig for survivors until further notice.

Every minute was frantic. A million problems and a million questions to be answered. I was in constant contact with the triage director, Dr. Lovit. Eighteen living people were dug out from under the piles of bricks, cement, and white powdery drywall.

The ambulance had carried a bomb, that much was perfectly clear. Those who were near the ambulance were all dead. The farther away you went from where the ambulance had been, the less extensive the wounds. The forty or so survivors from the ER had serious injuries. Twelve operating rooms were operational and had a constant flow of victims. Only two died while undergoing surgery. Those in the adjacent structures, most of them, were sent to our makeshift minor surgery center. Our New ER and minor surgery set-up was extremely efficient and operating smoothly, but still we were overwhelmed.

Again I called the hospital operator, this time to tell her, "Put us on bypass. We're accepting no new patients other than those injured by the bomb. Send them to Duke or UNC. Notify all the first responders."

Chapter 4

Pathology
Jackson City Hospital
2:31 p.m.

"From what I've seen, I may be the busiest doctor on the staff."

It was Dr. Sam Wilson, Chief of Pathology, calling me from the lab. He lowered his voice slightly, and then said, quietly, "You must come to my office. Now."

He hung up.

The abrupt request stunned me. What did a doctor of the dead have to tell me that was so important I had to meet him in his own office? We'd been working the disaster for roughly four hours now and the word from the morgue was that there were ten intact bodies and parts of probably a dozen more that had to be pieced together before they could be identified. Six ER docs and eight nurses were still unaccounted for. But none of that would be reason for me to have to stop what I was doing and go down to the Pathology Lab.

I started to walk, then ran to Sam's office. When I opened his door and stepped inside, he was facing the wall, away from me, smoking his pipe. Sam was well aware that the hospital was a non-smoking campus, and this was the first time I'd seen him smoke here.

I interrupted his silence with, "Is everything okay?"

"No."

Sam had been the doctor who'd directed the recovery of an airplane crash outside Raleigh the previous year that had killed a hundred and thirty-six people. He was very efficient in examining mangled dead people. After a moment, he started: "It's not the people who were killed by the explosion that bothers me. It's the people who were already dead in that ambulance when it exploded."

"You'll have to explain that one."

He walked to his microscope and gestured for me to look. I complied, but the sight of the tissue under the microscope didn't enlighten me.

"So?"

"So the parts of people that were in that ambulance, and there had to be at least a dozen or more, were all dead when the bomb went off. You can tell by looking at the slides."

"Uh, okay," I said, still clueless, not knowing what response he was looking for.

He looked at me, squinted his eyes, and then looked away. He placed another slide under his microscope and I looked at it to be polite.

"That slide is a piece of liver from one of the 'already dead' people." He cleared his throat and then explained. "The liver shows pre-mortem destruction of liver cells. Similar findings were in the lungs and spleen as well as a few of the brains from the 'already dead.' These people were all sick, very sick, and had died some time before the ER bomb detonated. There were only two of those in the ambulance with sick internal organs that were actually killed by the explosion."

"Do you know why they were sick?"

"It could be only one thing. Ebola."

I froze. "I ... I beg your pardon?"

"Scott," he said, "you must quarantine the entire area. Don't allow anyone in or out of the hospital. Do you understand me? We have to call the CDC. You have to get in touch with The National Guard, the police, the Mayor's Office, everyone, and get them to isolate the entire hospital. They need to get barbed-fucking-razor wire out there, I'm not kidding, and fencing, and guard stations every fifty yards. No one, not one soul, in or out, unless we know about it."

"But Ebola isn't an airborne virus."

"Yes, in normal cases, but that's not what you've got here, now is it? A biological weapon just exploded on your doorstep, Scott. You don't know what you're dealing with here. Nobody does. Try pleading technicalities in front of the public, or worse, the Mayor."

Hospital Administrator's Offices
4:14 p.m.

MY PHONE, SET TO vibrate, buzzed in my pocket. I looked at the caller ID, It was General Perkins. Oh no, I thought.

Roy Perkins had been on TV a lot lately. At the hearings before Congress, he'd been billed as Deputy Director of National Intelligence, although he'd held a number of other positions over the last few years. He always sat in front of the congressional panels, testifying from behind a desk, with other bureaucratic-types handing him papers and conferring with him. He stood out, nevertheless, because of his uniform. Perkins was an Air Force officer by trade, one who'd worked his way into the civilian intelligence agencies, like so many others had. But unlike the others, he'd kept his uniform on. His blue Air Force suit, with its four, silver, general's stars, seemed a strange contrast to his enormous bald head and his college professor demeanor. He was indeed sometimes referred to by others in the military as an "academic." On CNN and elsewhere he was always referred to as *the* counter-insurgency, counter-terrorist guru in Washington.

I pressed the button on my phone and said, "Dr. James."

A nasally voice said, "Please hold for the Deputy Director."

"James?"

"Yes."

"What the fuck is going on down there?"

"I think Omar Farok is on the move again."

"No shit. Why didn't we know this?

"How the hell do I know? Listen, I'm not involved in any of this shit."

"Bullshit! You and your buddies are locked in a war with Omar Farok, right?"

"No! I'm not at a war with *anybody*. I've told you that!"

"I don't care! You two are the only link to Farok. Where the hell is Keyes? You two are mine, understand? I *own* you from now on. Don't go anywhere. Don't do anything. Don't—"

"*Go somewhere?* It's a prison camp here!"

"Do not leave that location unless you hear from me. And keep your phone on you at all times. I'm going to find out what the hell is going on."

He hung up.

The Helipad
Jackson City Hospital
8:01 p.m.

TWO US ARMY HELICOPTERS bearing the Red Cross insignia roared overhead, circled for a moment, and then one eased down to the helipad just outside the main hospital entrance.

I started to run to greet them, with the nursing supervisor in tow, but a man in army fatigues jumped from the helicopter, wildly waving his arms to stop us. "Go back! Get back! You're under quarantine!"

I stopped, came to my senses, then saw three people, dressed from head to toe in Hazmat suits. They looked almost like astronauts in their white "spacesuits." They stepped down from the roaring aircraft, and began unloading boxes of equipment.

The leader of the group walked to me and shouted in muffled but understandable words from his helmet: "Sorry to be so rude! But we don't want your virus put back on that helicopter! The pilot and his crew aren't suited-up! Where do you want us to set up our operation?"

The Chief of Nursing, Eileen Pettit, along with Sam Wilson, led the spacesuited Hazmat team to Pathology.

The CDC Operations Chief, Dr. Andy Reed, the one who had talked to me on the helipad, directed his personnel to set up their equipment, and then waved four doctors, six nurses, and me, to follow him to an office nearby.

After introductions, Reed outlined a strict and thorough protocol that began with isolation procedures for everyone exposed to the possible Ebola virus. Next, he requested that all exposed individuals have blood tests and their history of the exposure be recorded. He went on and on, as Pettit and I made calls to get people to assist the CDC with their tasks.

They'd come from Atlanta at the first moment of alert and were extremely well organized. During our talk, Reed's phone rang. I thought it would be difficult to speak on a tiny phone using his bulky gloves, and with his head enclosed in the astronaut-like helmet, but he did something that surprised me. He punched a button on his wrist to connect an in-the-helmet phone system. After a short conversation, he turned to Wilson and said, "Your diagnosis of Ebola is probably right. The pre-existing disease in the internal organs of those in the ambulance is consistent with Ebola. The electron microscope will be a definitive test. We'll have that in about three hours."

Reed made notes and hit me with questions I thought were irrelevant, but they were details he felt necessary to his work. During the interview, one of his Hazmat team came in and without saying a word, rolled up my sleeve, drew blood, then recorded my temperature with a patch placed on my forehead.

Then, as abruptly as Reed had arrived, he dismissed himself and went to Pathology.

The Jackson City Hospital
Midnight

BY MIDNIGHT, THE CDC had changed the look of the hospital. Forty rooms were selected for the quarantine, occupying half of the first floor and encompassing the Pathology department, OR, and administrative offices. Their engineers created a closed ventilation system so that the air in the quarantine unit did not mix with the rest of the hospital. They installed a futuristic-looking conveyor-belt-sterilizing-system, centrally located in the isolation unit. All clothing, instruments, sheets, pillows, and every item in the unit were sterilized before being re-used, as was everything that touched the nurses, doctors, and all the ancillary personnel that left the unit. The CDC erected another odd looking device that took up an entire patient room: a big blue contraption for sterilizing body waste. It reduced solid and liquid matter to dust particles and stored it in twenty-pound plastic bags.

I spent the night surveying the hospital progress. In the ER, they sifted through every piece of debris, still looking for bodies and body parts.

Shortly after midnight, my phone rang. It was Keyes, who was still near the blast zone. "Scott, I've got the FBI on the other line. They're making the local cops go over to the house."

Chapter 5

Day 2
Dr. James' Home
Jackson City
7:35 a.m.

THERE WAS A KNOCK at the door. Jakjak, who had the boys occupied with their RC cars in the hallway next to the front room, reached in and put his hand on his gun. "Yu boyz ste hea'."

Jakjak crept into the front room and peered out from behind the curtains. A SWAT team in protective armor and carrying assault weapons stood at the door.

Jakjak looked to the street and saw what looked like a dozen Jackson Police cars.

Something didn't look right. "What do you want?" Jakjak cried out.

"Open the door or we'll knock it down."

The moment Jakjak cracked the door slightly they piled in against him, knocking him to the floor. He felt them gang tackle him and then a hand reached in to strip his weapon from its holster. He could feel them pulling his arms back and cuffing his wrists.

"Wut haff I dun?! Wut are yu doing to me?!"

Scotty and Jeremy, the two boys, wandered into the front room and were grabbed and scooped up by heavily armed men in black. The boys began shrieking.

"What are you doing?!" Jakjak yelled.

One man lifted the visor from his face and in a loud voice, said, "We're relocating you! And good riddance as far as The City of Jackson is concerned! Bring up the van! Let's get these ... *people* ... out of here!"

Conference Room
Hospital Administrator's Offices
9:30 a.m.

DR. REED CALLED AND said that he wanted to update hospital leaders on his team's findings and give further instructions. I called the operator and had her contact the Executive Committee, a governing body comprised of the department heads, committee chairmen, and all the assistant hospital administrators quarantined in the hospital. The group assembled within fifteen minutes. The two from the CDC were the only ones in the room in spacesuits and helmets.

Dr. Reed gave his report: "Ebola virus was definitively diagnosed by electron microscopy." Everyone groaned, even though they knew before this report came in that it was Ebola. Then, he gave what he called the "good news."

The vast majority of the patients who had been in the hospital at the time of the explosion, as well as most of the doctors, nurses, and people in maintenance and facilities, were not exposed and could be released from quarantine to return to their homes. I began to applaud and the other members of the executive committee followed.

Reed was resuming his talk when my telephone rang. I looked to see that the caller was the Mayor's Office. I answered in a quiet voice, "Dr. James."

It was Mayor LaShaun Washington. "I know you are in a meeting with Dr. Reed and your staff. I'm going to call back in a minute on Skype so I can teleconference with your entire group."

I paused for a moment to comprehend his demand, and hung up. I opened Skype on my computer. The large screen at the end of conference room went from black to a picture of Mayor Washington and a group of people sitting at a conference table.

The Mayor spoke: "Dr. James, you will recognize everyone in my panel, the Jackson City City Council, and of course the City Attorney, Ms. Marks.

"Dr. James. This conference is called into emergency session. Now, let's get right to the point: Dr. James, did you receive a message from a terrorist group that mentioned 'Ebola'?"

"What?"

"Dr. James: Did you, or did you not, receive a message from a known terrorist organization in the last twenty-four hours? The Jackson City Police have the article in their possession. You are a terrorist. You affiliate with terrorists, you've been the center of multiple attacks, and why the FBI has allowed you to carry on, purely in the interest of having another informant—"

"I am not a terrorist, sir!"

"Dr. James—you are out of order here. This is an emergency meeting. Let's get to the second point, of which this body has just been informed: You are immune to Ebola. Is that correct?"

"What?"

Reed stepped forward and said through his mask, "We have not informed Dr. James of that yet. We just got the results. Frankly I'm a little shocked that *you* know."

"I assure you Dr. Reed, this body *will* be involved in every aspect of this ongoing tragedy. Dr. James, we find it all just a little too convenient that the epidemic you have created here in the United States is something that you also just happen to be immune to—"

"I didn't *create* anything!" I screamed. "What are you talking about! It's Omar Farok! He's doing all this!"

"Dr. James! That's enough! That is enough! That is *enough!* Now … The FBI will be taking you into custody shortly. We are cooperating thoroughly in their investigation. This body is going to make sure that the federal authorities do the right thing and indict you for conspiracy. You are directly responsible for a number of terrorist attacks and your connection with certain cults is well known. The City Council has passed a binding resolution that relieves you of your position at The Jackson City Hospital. *Permanently*. We are also considering civil action against you and your *group*."

"Why don't you just banish me from the city! You're a dictator, right?"

"Dr. James."

"Just throw me out of my own home! You *are* a dictator, right?"

"Dr. James. That's enough."

I turned and looked at the scornful stares of my hospital staff. Many of these doctors had been my friends for many years. I had grown up with so many of them. But no one spoke a word in my defense.

Hallway
Jackson City Hospital
10:02 a.m.

I WALKED SLOWLY DOWN the hall with Reed by my side. "Sorry about what happened to you in there," he said. "I didn't know you were going to be blindsided."

Then, there was a long pause. He looked like he had a lot on his mind that he wasn't telling me.

I can't stand someone who starts to tell me something and then takes all day to say it.

At last, he continued. "Your antibody IgG and IgM titers are positive."

What the hell are antibody IgG and IgM titers? I thought. Thankfully, I didn't say that.

After what seemed like another long pause, he continued. "Those antibodies are present in individuals who have acquired resistance to the Ebola virus."

"Does that mean I'm a carrier of Ebola or that I'm immune to the disease?"

"Immune. You're being released. Immediately, I'm afraid." He sensed my lack of understanding of the terms and continued, "In the ELISA test, the Enzyme Linked Immuno Sorbent Assay, the sides of the tubes are coated with a specific viral antigen for the Zaire Ebola Virus, then the tube is exposed to the serum on the person studied, and evaluated six hours later. If the immune globulin G adheres to the coating, it proves either an immunity to Ebola or an early infection."

"How do you tell the difference?"

"Your exposure was only eleven hours ago, and it takes more than four days after exposure before the titers begin to rise. You were exposed only eleven hours ago."

"But, still, how can you be sure which it is?"

"Well, your titers were high, fourteen hundred. In the early stages of the disease it's a hundred or less. One thousand or greater titers come only after being exposed for periods of two weeks, and over a thousand? If you've got over a thousand with the active Ebola disease, you'd be dead."

"So tell me what that all means."

"It means that you were exposed to either the disease or to immune serum before the blast, and your immune titer is very high. You won't get Ebola."

I thought for a second before saying, "What a deal: I'm free from the disease. Now I'll be released from quarantine so the Mayor can deport me to Kalamazoo."

"I haven't finished yet. There's more good news."

"The Mayor dropped dead of a heart attack."

"Ha, ha. No. Even better. One other individual we tested also bears the antibodies. Elizabeth Keyes."

Chapter 6

Quarantine Exit Corridor
Jackson City Hospital
11:15 a.m.

Walk through. Disrobe completely. Walk forward.
Spray wash. Walk forward. Wash more thoroughly. Walk
forward. Answer questions. Walk forward.

Suddenly I was on the outside of the quarantine, in a
portable building, awaiting the FBI. I figured it would be
the same guys I'd dealt with before. The attendant directed
me to a room and told me to wait.

After just a moment, the door opened and in walked
a man I'd never seen before. He reached out his hand.
"Hello, I'm Andy Reed."

I looked at this man, over six feet, thin, with a blond
crew cut and ruddy complexion, in his early 30s, wearing

a seersucker sport coat and a red bow tie. I realized that I'd only seen him in his Hazmat suit and had no idea what he looked like in real life. For a person of such enormous responsibility, he was very warm. I reached out and shook his hand, "You seem a little under-dressed without your spacesuit."

He smiled and sat down. "Dr. James, we're in a hurry here, so let me get started: I need to learn where you acquired this immunity."

"I have no idea. I haven't been anywhere near Africa. The only Ebola epidemic was in Africa, correct? The one that killed several thousand people. Is that still active?"

"Yes and no. That was in Sierra Leone and Guinea. It peaked eight months ago with more than four thousand cases, but that outbreak totally subsided. Occasionally there is a case, but the world is currently free of the disease, more or less. Until now."

"Where did it originate?"

"Along the Ebola River in Zaire, now the Republic of the Congo, in 1976. It was dormant until it sprang up again in the Congo in 1995, then Uganda in 2000, and then the recent Sierre Leone epidemic. I'm trying to equate our virus to one of those outbreaks, which is just beginning to grow in the laboratory here. We haven't pinned down the type as of yet."

"Then the present virus will be named the Jackson City virus."

He laughed. "Or the Scott James virus."

I don't know why I found this humorous in the present situation, but I laughed.

"Each time there has been an epidemic, Scott, it's gotten worse. The '76 epidemic had 109 cases, the one in '95, 315, in 2000, there were 425 cases, and in 2015, 4000 cases."

"Okay. So you're saying that if it continues its trend, there will likely be a lot more here than in past epidemics."

"That's what we believe right now, yes. Now, let's get on with the questions and answers."

He asked about my travels in the past year, which was easy. I was surprised at his questions about the animals I'd contacted and the animal meat I'd consumed in Haiti and Fiji. Apparently, monkeys, chimps, and apes carry the disease and eating their flesh has been attributed to the transmission of Ebola. Strains of bats in Africa also carry the disease, many times for long periods of time without becoming infected.

Afterward, after he'd narrowed down some of the possibilities with a few questions, he was quiet for a moment. Then he said, "Dr. James, uhm, I know about your background, your *reputation*, if you will. I've talked to General Perkins, or perhaps I should say he talked to me. He said that you've been involved with zombies, that you know a lot about zombie-ism."

I didn't know where this was going. I answered slowly, "Yes. I guess you could say that. In a manner of speaking."

"So, tell me about that."

"What does that have to do with anything?"

"There are only two people involved in this affair who are immune to Ebola, you and Elizabeth Keyes. You two do dabble in zombie-ism, correct? Isn't that what the Mayor was talking about? Cultism? The fact that the two of you had Ebola immunity is not happenstance. There was an occurrence, to both of you, that made you immune. And, I might add, that as high as your IgG titer was, hers was even higher, 2000."

"I don't '*dabble* in zombie-ism.' That's Perkins talking. I know a priestess in Haiti."

"The zombie queen. What's her name?"

"That's what Perkins calls her, 'zombie queen.' Her real name is Sanfia. She has, I guess, what you could call kind of a 'zombie army.'"

"The 'zombie queen,'" he said, slowly, "has a 'zombie army.'"

"Not exactly. Sanfia is the most powerful woman in Haiti, but she operates underground. She is a Vodoun priestess. She knows how to make people into zombies. She uses drugs, like scopolomine and extract from sea cucumber, bufotoxin and tetrodotoxin, to put people into a deep fugue state. That's what zombies really are—people in a deep trance-like state who are susceptible to suggestion. She can make these people do anything she wants."

"You live in an interesting world, Dr. James."

"I don't *live* in any *world,* Dr. Reed—I was dragged into it by Omar Farok. This is all Farok's doing. He wants to kill me and probably kill Keyes, too."

"Yes, Perkins said something like that. Why does a terrorist want to kill you?"

"Revenge. I guess he thinks he has to prove something. He's insane. He's completely insane. And *rich*, filthy rich."

"Tell me about what happened in Haiti."

"I was trying to find out about an operation that Farok was planning to carry out against America. Keyes and I penetrated a Vodoun Society, a Sanpwel, to get information. My friend, Jakjak, was a member. But we got caught. Sanfia tried to make us into zombies. They struck both of our heads with stones and rubbed Sanfia's zombie potion on our open wounds. I dodged the blow to my head, and I took the antidote immediately. Keyes got it bad. Her head had the deeper wound. There was a delay before I could get her the antidote."

"That's it. She had a larger wound on her head. She absorbed more of the antibody or antigens from the zombie poison and therefore has a higher antibody titer. Did you see this Sanfia mix the zombie formula?"

"No. I doubt anyone ever has."

"Well, it doesn't matter. That's the answer. I'm sure of it. She used animal blood, or some kind of cadaverous material, to mix up the stuff she gave you. Could be bat's blood, maybe ape's. Who knows, maybe human blood. Whatever it was it contained enough antibody to make you immune."

There was a knock at the door, and then it opened slowly. It was Keyes, looking perplexed.

"I believe we've already met. I'm Andy Reed."

"I didn't recognize you." She shook his hand reticently, then looked at me and said, "Scott, do you know about the immunity?"

"Dr. Reed here believes it came from the zombie poison. Sanfia may have mixed it up in a solution of infected blood."

She sat down next to me, and Reed said, "I need your immune serum to give to any of the people in the hospital who develop the first symptoms of Ebola. Thirty-six percent of your blood is serum and that serum is what carries the immune globulins. That's what will help to convey immunity to others, your blood ..."

Keyes listened patiently.

"You draw the blood," he went on, "you let it clot, and then you centrifuge away the blood cells. The rest is serum. With—"

Keyes interrupted. "You draw the blood into a container with an anticoagulant, centrifuge it to rid it of all red and white blood cells, and the liquid is plasma."

"Uh, yes. General Perkins told me you are unusually 'well-informed.' The immune serum is one of the agents that has been used in the seven Ebola cases treated in America. Other agents used were the drugs Brincido Fovir, TKM-Ebola, and ZMapp, an antibody preparation."

"What happened to those people?"

"There were two deaths, one in Texas, but the man wasn't diagnosed until the ninth day after exposure. The second was in Nebraska, again nine days after exposure. The other five with Ebola still live, disease free."

"What was their treatment regimen?" I asked.

"All agents were in short supply, so there was a mixture of drugs used in the group, but all received immune serum, like the two of you have."

"Which of the drugs you mentioned will be used here?"

"I've already made the calls, and there aren't enough of any of them to treat our patients here."

"How far will Keyes' and my serum go?"

"Serum comprises thirty-six percent of the blood volume. Yours," he pointed to me, "will be two liters and Ms. Keyes', 1.8 liters."

"How much is used per patient?"

"Depends. In some patients, as much as 400 cc, divided into three doses, two days apart. In others, only 200 cc have been given. With the variability of doses given, and the variability of other drugs given these same patients, it's impossible to say which drugs, along with how much serum, created the cure."

"So where does that leave us?"

"The blood serum between the two of you will only treat about thirteen people. To even give the smaller amount of serum, 200 cc per person in divided doses, to the ones who might be infected here, we have to have a minimum of sixty-two liters of blood."

"That's a lot of donors."

"We'd need at least thirty-one, if we draw blood twice, but it would be better to have fifty or sixty. And that means we're going to have to go to Haiti and find Sanfia."

"We?"

"You're the one, Dr. James. You have to come with me to talk to these people and see if we can find others who are immune."

"The only way to do that is through Jakjak. We have to have Jakjak. He's the only one who can get into the underground societies there."

"Where is he?"

"In police protection. Maybe the FBI. My kids have been hauled away, too."

"Alright. I'll call General Perkins. We'll get Jakjak."

"I'll give you my blood, so long as a drop of it never gets to Mayor Washington."

Reed looked at me.

"Just kidding."

Keyes and I rolled up our sleeves as a young nurse dressed in a white lab coat came in and placed IV needles in our arms.

"Sorry about the Mayor kicking us out of town," Keyes said

I stiffened.

"I've been reading his e-mail. He's been working on burying you for a while."

"Great."

"I've been working the Internet. I can't find Farok on any of his sites or chat rooms, not even the dark ones. He's changed all his banks and shows no open contacts with his financial institutions or his donors."

"Maybe he's changed all his passwords."

"No, it's more than that. He's doing something really weird. I can feel it."

Chapter 7

The Hilton Hotel
Jackson City
2:42 p.m.

WE'D BEEN ESCORTED BACK to the house, to get a few personal things, and then they'd hurried us to downtown Jackson City, where Perkins and his staff had evidently set up shop in a hotel room.

When we got there, Dr. Reed answered the door. "There are a few glitches," he said as he ushered us in.

"Where are my kids, Reed? They wouldn't tell me."

"Everything's okay, Dr. James." Perkins said, walking into the room. He seemed slightly disheveled, like he had put on his uniform in a hurry. "I've been on the phone with the FBI. They know how to handle this stuff. Everything's going to be fine. They drove your boys up to Quantico. They're safe. They have people with them. You can talk to them right now, if you want."

I walked in to see that Jakjak was sitting by himself on a couch in the main room, looking bewildered. "*Dokte*," he said, "De took us in handcuffs. De came in de house really ruff and took us to the police station."

My heart sank. The Mayor had gone too far.

"Just calm down," Perkins said, looking at my reaction, "I've been apprised of the situation since it began. Mayor Washington was a bit abrupt, and his police force doesn't pay attention to the current public reaction to police brutality. They were a little rough on your family. But I am not the one to apologize for that. Now, have a cup of coffee, Dr. James, or for those who wish, a little Vodka Collins."

He shook the ice cubes in his clear liquid beverage, and then cleared his throat. "I'm going to have my assistant take notes." He called out, "Lieutenant Moss, come and take notes."

A shapely young lady in military dress came in. She looked like an athlete of some sort, tanned and angular. She and General Perkins smiled very warmly at each other.

Keyes and I sat down on the couch, next to Jakjak.

"There's a problem here, Dr. James, and I think you know what it is," Perkins said. He looked in his drink, took a sip, and placed the glass on the coffee table. He cleared his throat as he leaned toward us. "Your voodoo queen died thirty years ago. We've known this for a while, but we didn't care, until now."

Jakjak's eyes widened. "No suh. She ees as alive as you and me."

The general took a photograph from a folder on his desk. "This is a photograph taken of the then twenty-five year-old Angelique Sanfina, who is referenced as Sanfia, when she entered a Haitian prison in 1970. It's strongly rumored that the Duvaliers, Papa Doc and Baby Doc, had a prison under the National Palace while they were in power, but that it was closed after their rule ended. We believe she was in that prison."

Jakjak and I looked at the picture. I saw a slight resemblance between this woman and the elderly Sanfia I had once encountered, but not much more. Jakjak positively identified the pictured woman as Sanfia. "It's for sure the Sanfia that saved my life while I was there. She ees much older now, but that's her, as she looked when I first met her, years ago."

"How sure?" General Perkins asked.

"One hundred percent."

The general thumbed through some papers and read from a Haitian newspaper dated October 25, 1971. "Baby Doc Duvalier executed thirty prisoners for insurgency." He thumbed down the list of names and read, "Angelique Sanfina is listed here. This photo was taken when she entered prison in July, 1970. And there are photos given here of all the rest of those later executed. We think they were all the ones in the underground prison."

He passed the newspaper article with the photos to Jakjak.

Jakjak shook his head. "I don't know any of the others, but this ees Sanfia. She ees a lot olda now, but that's her."

I studied the photo in the newspaper. The resemblance was unmistakable. I thought for a minute. "She knew the jail beneath the National Palace in Haiti quite well, and said she'd attended to those imprisoned there for a number of years. So maybe she escaped the execution and lived on?"

The General sorted through more papers and laid on the table three photographs of the same woman, looking very dead with a gunshot wound in the middle of her chest. "The CIA had these."

Jakjak looked at me. "That ees Sanfia. But I know she's alive."

"My sources say there is no Angelique Sanfina in Haiti. This is a part of your story that frankly never checked out, Dr. James. We let it go because, well, who cares about zombies? But now that we've got this ... situation, it's different."

I shook my head. "But I was at one of their Bizango Society meetings. Sanfia was the big dog of the group. The police Chief of Port au Prince was there, and the governors of the provinces, and all of them held offices in Sanfia's Society, didn't they Jakjak?"

"*O wi, Doktè*, they are all Présidentes of my, or what used to be my Sanpwel."

There was silence. Perkins stood and walked around the room. The General's face slowly turned red. Lieutenant Moss followed him around the room with adoring eyes. "Either you people are pulling some kind of shit on me, or Angelique Sanfina is alive, or she's dead, or there's someone masquerading as her in Port au Prince, or I don't know."

He stopped and looked at me.

"Either way, you guys are going to go to Haiti with Reed. You're going to get inside the societies, and you're going to find out what they gave you that caused you to have immunity."

Jakjak scowled. "The society will make me into a zombie if I go back, and that's a lot worse than any punishment you can give me. I'd rather be hanged than be made into a zombie by my own people."

General Perkins looked at Jakjak. "Frankly I don't believe that. I am tired of all this zombie talk. Tell me what's worse: Being a free zombie, or being in jail the rest of your life?"

Jakjak stood and looked hard at Perkins. "I talked to zombies before. Dey say de experience in de coffin before they let out seem like a thousand years. De remember every minute of the horror of breathing hard for a little air, de pain in de lungs, and de pain all over de bodies as de gasp for breath. Dying is painful, and they die for a long, long time, hundreds of years in that twenty-four hours before de're dug up. De come out of de coffin as slaves of their master. De are whipped and de hurt worse than you or I would hurt, but de brain won't allow them to complain, de just hurt and stay quiet. De are in constant hunger, but de stomach knots up and de can't swallow food. De want to die. De cut themselves, but de don't bleed. De jump off high buildings and feel every bit of the pain, for years and years, even after de bones have healed. De try to hang themselves, but de bodies don't need much oxygen and de live and hurt until someone cuts dem down, even days later."

General Perkins swallowed, then said, calmly, "Okay. Alright. But what can we do if this Sanfia can't be found?"

I spoke. "But she's there. Jakjak knows people in the

societies and the houses she owns and the places she keeps her zombie labor force. Jakjak, we have to penetrate the group to find her."

Jakjak shrugged. He was always brave, but I knew this was almost too much to ask. "I now an outsider. Maybe nobody talk to me. Maybe de try to make me a zombie. If de think I reveal the secret Bizango Societies to the outside world, de kill me."

"I need you to arrange for the FBI and CIA to assist Keyes," I said to Perkins. "We need her here, working the Internet, at least for the time being. Getting the serum may not be enough. We have to know what Omar Farok is planning."

"Yes, yes," Perkins said. "I'll arrange that. I have as much interest in locating Omar Farok as you, and my people working in cooperation with Ms. Keyes will find him this time. Lieutenant Moss, let's have the ... the ... *pills.*"

He turned and looked at Reed and me and became very stern. "I'm sure you two know about the efforts of law enforcement to track controlled substances, especially stuff like oxycontin."

"They put tiny GPS tracking chips in the prescription bottles."

"Correct," Perkins said, as he extracted three prescription bottles from a small brown case.

"So you want to track us through these bottles," I said.

Perkins started to smile, widely, wickedly, and then opened one of the bottles so that we could see a tiny piece of green plastic, sitting at the bottom. "No. Lt. Moss here is going to inject this mean little bastard into your butt."

Moss started preparing a pneumatic syringe, like the type used for mass-inoculations.

"Eh ... Gee, Perkins ... I don't know ... "

"Dr. James, I own you. If I want to shoot a stump up your ass, I can. We've been able to keep a lid on your *activities* thus far, but that's gone. Mayor Washington and every other politician in the country wants you handed over to the FBI for conspiracy, aiding and abetting known terrorist organizations, and the list just goes on. They want your head, understand? I am the only thing keeping you and your *friends* out of a federal penitentiary right now, and I'm not letting you out of my sight." He smiled, again very wickedly. He was enjoying this. "Now, pull down your pants, James. I hope this hurts like hell."

"You don't have to shoot me in the ass with that thing, Perkins. You could just put it in my arm."

"Eh, maybe. But we've found that right below the gluteus maximus is the last place people look." He tilted his glass back and took a long drink, then gestured to Jakjak and Reed. "So, all of you chumps: Bottoms up."

Chapter 8

Airport
Homestead Airbase, Florida
7:50 p.m.

THE AIR FORCE TRANSPORT touched down after a short flight, and I awoke to Perkins talking to Reed in the seats behind me. "There's good news. The State Department has spoken to President Longpre of Haiti. He's cooperating. However, there is some … trouble … on the ground. The local security forces are stirring up some problems. I've arranged to get you extra air capability, as well as a little extra help on your security detail. We have a lot of people on the ground, working earthquake relief. The Army has an infantry unit with an aviation regiment doing their deployment. They're a National Guard unit from Florida.

Good soldiers, all of them. They've done escort duty all over. Convoys. Lots of them. And lots of medivac stuff."

"But they're reservists? You mean they're only there for a week?"

"Officially these people have about eleven days before they're out. I don't think that's going to be a factor. It is my understanding of our present situation that if you and James don't get a whole hell of lot of blood serum in the next eleven days, it won't really matter a whole hell of a lot for those poor souls back at the quarantine. Am I right?"

"I guess you're right," Reed said.

"And these guys are nearby. I'm having two helicopters sent over to where you're going to set up. They'll be coming over with a squad of infantry, to help with security. I've also arranged to have a couple of squads of infantry on stand by, if you need it. The guy in charge of your detail is named Roberts. He's a captain. He flies one of the birds. He's the guy you talk to. They'll meet you at the airport."

"What about the Marines at the embassy?"

"No. We don't want to pull anybody off the embassy. Things are too hot on the ground right now. We want to keep them there unless things change. I'll call President Longpre and tell him to expect you in the morning."

"No, no," Reed said. "We need to go tonight. Further delay could be disastrous. Can't our flight just go on to Haiti?"

General Perkins snapped his fingers and Lt. Moss popped into the cabin. She seemed flushed, like she'd just been running.

"Get President Longpre on the line again."

Lt. Moss dialed and got an immediate response. She stuck her head in and said, "The President is on the line."

"Mr. President. Sir, the urgency of finding the Ebola cure necessitates our team coming tonight. They'll be there in two-to-three hours."

Longpre said, "They'll need an escort. I'll send our National Police."

He abruptly hung up before General Perkins could say more.

I looked at Perkins for a moment. Something didn't smell right to me.

"He says he wants you guys to use a police escort."

General Perkins looked at the floor and mumbled unintelligibly. He stood and walked around the cabin for a minute. Then he leaned toward Reed and said, in a soft tone, "I have to stay here, at Homestead. They're setting up an office for me here. The embassy people and the Haitian Government will be handling you in-country. It's going to be a little hot on the ground. Don't go anywhere without the National Police escort. And don't piss them off. They have a reputation for brutality and no one, not even President Longpre, has control over them. I'll call Ambassador Farmer and have him meet you at the airport. Be careful around the Police."

Chapter 9

Toussaint Louverture International Airport
Port au Prince
11:39 p.m.

ON THE FLIGHT FROM Homestead, I had a lot of time to think. Everything was now all clear to me. I'd been a fugitive since the fight between me and Omar Farok began. I'd been on the run. I'd dodged bullets, terrorist bombs, fists, zombie poisons, even sharks. I would remain a fugitive until I did something to change that. I wanted my freedom again, like I had before all this mess began, freedom to do my plastic surgery and take care of my kids ... and maybe even Elizabeth Keyes. And I wanted this more than life itself.

But how?

As we landed, we looked out the windows of our plane to see that we were surrounded by the blue suited, Haitian National Police, probably fifty of them. Behind us, two US Army helicopters had just landed, and we could see that this was our security detail. But something was clearly wrong. The Haitian police were swarming around our plane aggressively. It wasn't just their presence that intimidated us. It was the snub-nosed pistols that were attached to black, plastic stocks that they carried like rifles. They held the guns to their faces, continually aiming at us.

"Jesus Christ," Reed said.

Reed's phone buzzed. "This is Dr. Reed."

"Dr. Reed, this is Michael Barnes, I am the Ambassador's assistant. Get your security detail the hell out of here. *Please,* do not have your people displaying any of their weapons. The local security are always looking for a fight and there's nobody in this country who can control them. Your security detail's weapons are a lot better than their Heckler & Koch pistols on rifle stocks, and yours are full auto, and either they'll be happy to confiscate them for themselves or there will be a fire fight. They're probably going to start a fire fight anyway. Now get those people out of here!"

"I haven't even met them yet! I wouldn't know who to call!"

"Tell the pilot of your aircraft to tell them to leave! Tell them!"

We could see the doors of the helicopters opening and the squad of infantry starting to dismount.

Reed started shouting up to cockpit, "Hey! Do you have those guys on frequency?"

The two helmeted pilots turned slowly and looked at Reed. One nodded his head, perplexed.

"Well, tell them to get the hell out of here before they start a war with the locals! Tell them to go to the staging area right now! Tell them to leave!"

The two pilots looked at each other, then the copilot looked back and nodded. He began talking into his mic. We couldn't hear what he was saying, but it was clear that the pilot of the helicopter was arguing with him.

After a moment, the helicopter doors pulled closed and the two choppers slowly lifted off the ground and disappeared into the night.

It took us a few moments to gather our gear and get organized, and then Reed took a deep breath and nodded to the young crewman of our plane to open the door.

As we came out, the Haitians mobbed us. We could barely walk down the stairs from the plane. The feeling of claustrophobia was intense. We had to push our way through huge, blue suited men.

We could see Ambassador Farmer, whom Perkins had said would be there, blocked behind the mass of police, trying to push his way through to get to us. We were being pushed and shoved and pressed. I called out, "Please let the Ambassador get through! Let him through!"

Nobody responded.

Jakjak called out in his native language, "*Tanpri, kite anbasadè a. Tanpri, kite anbasadè a.*"

The crowd seemed to give a little, and Farmer pushed through to us. He was sweating as he shook our hands and introduced himself. "I'm Farmer. We have to get out of here. The situation is very precarious."

"Don't you have security?" I asked.

"No. They're really touchy about that right now. President Longpre and his buddies don't like the idea of you guys doing anything with Ebola in their country. They claim we're violating their sovereignty."

The police mob opened a slim pathway and our party of twelve CDC scientists, lead by Ambassador Farmer and his assistant, slowly snaked its way to two passenger vans. The police stayed circled around our group, tightly forming a moving cocoon. After the van doors closed, Reed looked at Farmer and said, "This is insane."

Secure Housing Unit
Quantico, VA.
11:39 p.m.

KEYES FINALLY ARRIVED AFTER a short flight and a lengthy briefing by the Special Agent In Charge. Afterward, she was taken to a dismal looking apartment complex near the headquarters, and introduced to her minder, Special Agent Jane Hopkins.

Jane's attractive face and slim, tall body were burdened by her bun-rolled, salt and pepper hair, frumpy clothes, old lady shoes, a rigidly erect posture, and annoying demeanor.

"I need a secure line," Keyes said, after a cold handshake, "to call Dr. Scott James."

"Oh, now, now, Honey, we all want something in life, but we don't always get it. Before you talk to your ... uh

... your *cohorts*, you're going to sit here and find out what the hell is going on."

Keyes sat at a computer that only the world's largest intelligence-gathering conglomerate could create. Keyes clenched her teeth and muttered under her breath, "My *cohorts* have saved you're ass about ten times, bitch."

"I beg your pardon?"

Elizabeth frowned, then re-grouped herself. "What about the kids? Where are Jeremy and Scotty?"

"I'm sure you won't be disappointed. The kids like movies, and their sixty-inch TV has Netflix, all the movies they could ever want. Tutors start with Scotty and Jeremy tomorrow, one on one."

"Assure me, they'll be safe."

"Honey, this is Quantico, the safest place on Earth."

"I want to see them."

"Well, we'll see about that, now won't we?"

Chapter 10

Temporary Headquarters of the CDC Team
Haiti
1:05 a.m.

WE DROVE TO A small lot of concrete and overgrown grass. You got the feeling that the Haitian and American governments had agreed to keep this whole "outbreak thing" low key, far from a centralized location, tucked away. The lot consisted of a spacious but ancient parking lot that stretched from the street to two, steel, nondescript Quonset huts, with round roofs.

The first of the rickety structures was filled with fifty cots in a community living area. I looked in the one restroom and saw a single shower, one commode, and one urinal.

The second Quonset was totally empty save for a chalk board, a dozen wooden folding chairs, and two plastic-wrapped pallets of equipment that had just been delivered. *Hmm. These are the special arrangements for us?*

Reed barked out commands and his CDC staff began to set up their lab equipment. He directed that the Command Quonset be divided into a lab and a staging area, and then sent one of the vans back to the airport to get a load of gear off of the plane.

Amid all the commotion of setting up, a tall, good-looking man, wearing a green helmet and fatigues, walked into the Command Quonset. He had a neatly trimmed, regulation-issue mustache, and a slightly wild look in his eye. He walked up to me and said, "Dr. James, I'm Roberts. This is staff sergeant Manthripagada." He gestured to a compact guy with dark brown skin and a crew cut. He looked second-generation Indian or maybe Sri Lankan. The individual black letters of his enormous last name had been printed so closely together on his uniform that you could barely tell them apart.

"How are you, Captain Roberts, and Sergeant ... uh ... forgive me."

The sergeant looked a little wild, too, and cocky. He smiled a wide grin of blazing white teeth. "'Sarge' is fine."

"Sarge."

"That'll do for now."

"Okay, Sarge, Captain Roberts, you guys have been briefed on the evolving situation, right?" I pointed in the direction of where the Haitian police mob had parked most of their cars, on the outskirts of our little compound. "Try to keep any display of hardware under wraps. This is supposed to be a medical mission."

"We understand. We're going to stay with the birds."

"Take these," Sarge said, handing me two, hand-held radios. "I've already set these up for you guys. We monitor the frequency, 24/7." He looked at me for moment, then flashed that cocky smile of his, and said, "If you guys get into any shit, you call me and the Captain immediately, right?"

"Understood."

Temporary Headquarters of the CDC Team
1:45 a.m.

JAKJAK LEFT IN ONE of the vans with a driver from the embassy. He knew that the best way to make contact with Sanfia was discreetly, alone.

They drove slowly toward the police ring, flashed their lights, and were allowed to pass.

But the police followed them. Like a smothering cloak.

Three cars stayed on their tail. Only a few blocks away from the CDC compound, Jakjak finally stopped the van, got out, then yelled, "*Rete! Se pou ou kite nou al sèlman.* Stop! Let us go alone!"

It was no use. They ignored his words. Jakjak was back in less than twenty minutes. He came walking up to Reed and me, flustered. "I can't do dis with all those police. It'll scare Sanfia and we'll never get to speak to her."

"What if we just fly out?" I said to Reed. "Just take a chopper to some place and get a car?"

"No. Absolutely not. Perkins said we have to.stay with the police."

I took Jakjak aside to discuss the situation. Jakjak had a certain genius for planning. I had never, in fact, seen a jam that he couldn't get out of. We walked outside and looked out toward the street and the mob of police. "How are we going to shake our police escort?" I asked.

"We create de distraction."

"How do we do that?"

He looked out on the mob for a moment, then said. "Alcohol."

Chapter 11

Temporary Headquarters of the CDC Team
2:00 a.m.

AFTER TWO RINGS, AN official voice answered, saying, "United States Embassy. This is Michael Barnes speaking."

"Michael! Scott James here! *Doctor* ... Scott James. How are ya! I hope I'm not calling you too late there fella!"

"Uh, well, no. We've been pretty busy here at the embassy. We're still handling the arrangements for you guys."

"You guys are doing a fine job. I mean that! Really! A fine job! There's just one thing: I was wondering if perhaps we could get some supplies out here, especially some food, maybe even a little beer."

"Beer?"

"Yeah! You know. *Beer.*"

"Uh ... Well, we had made arrangements for the food service people to be out there in a few hours to serve breakfast, but ..."

"Yes, we know that, but, well, you know, we're trying to cheer things up a little. It's been an exhausting few days, and I just thought you guys might be able to send over some food right now. Just anything would be good. Don't you guys have a cafeteria?"

"Uhm, well. The cafeteria is mostly closed right now. Let me see, maybe we can have something—"

"It would mean a lot. Really. You guys do have *beer*, right?"

"Yes ... There is some in the warehouse ... It's mainly for the Marine's mess. But, uh ... "

"Great! We're going to send your driver over there right now to pick up whatever you've got. We're trying to cheer the place up a little, if you know what I mean."

Jakjak and I went back inside and gave Reed the happy news. "Dr. Reed, I've just talked to the ambassador's assistant, Barnes. He says he has some food for us. You know, from the embassy cafeteria, potato salad and that sort of thing."

Reed frowned. "Right now? Potato salad? I thought they weren't coming until 6:00 am."

"Nah. He *insists* that we send one of the vans over there right now to pick it up."

Chapter 12

Temporary Headquarters of the CDC Team
2:45 a.m.

THE VAN RETURNED FROM the embassy and backed up to the little cement dock next to the forward Quonset hut. I "volunteered" to unload it by myself. I opened the back doors of the van and hurriedly stacked the warm, insulated catering containers on the cement, and then handed Jakjak two cases of Miller beer.

When I'd dropped the last box, and Jakjak was ready, I called out to the embassy driver, who was sitting at the wheel of the idling van, "Hey, buddy, can you give me a hand with this?"

Jakjak stepped out from behind the van and started trotting across the parking lot with the two cases of beer in his arms. He hurried down to the far corner of the parking lot and then called out to the police, "*Byè pou tout moun!* Beer for everyone!"

As the embassy driver was getting out, I walked forward, past him, and said, "There's some stuff I can't lift. Can you get somebody to help us? I'll be right back."

Confused, the driver, who looked like a clerk who'd been wrangled into driving duty, said, "Uh ... " and then disappeared behind the van.

I saw the police starting to congregate around the beer, and then Jakjak took off running. I jumped in the van, threw it in gear, and then accelerated right into a block of yellow painted concrete that was once a parking space marker. The van jumped into the air violently and I hit my head on the roof. Jakjak was sprinting toward me and I could see that the only way to pick him up was on my side. Pushing the driver's side door open, I yelled, "Come on, man! Run! Come on!"

He flung himself onto the opened door and I aimed the speeding van for a spot between the police cars that was just big enough for us to snake through. The police were already running to their cars, shouting. Some stayed behind with the beer and seemed to be scuffling and fighting over it.

We passed through the parked cars and then Jakjak started shouting, "Leff! Turn leff, *Dokte*! Leff!"

We barely made the turn and then he shouted, "All de way down and turn right!"

We raced through the backstreets for a few minutes with Jakjak precariously hanging onto my door, and then we knew we'd lost them.

We stopped, Jakjak let himself down off the door, and then said, panting and stretching out his exhausted limbs, "We have to go to some houses and get some information."

Chapter 13

Backstreets of Port au Prince
3:00 a.m.

JAKJAK DROVE US TO a friend's home, a ramshackle, cement block structure at the end of a crumbling street. He got out in the darkness and then knocked quietly on the door. There was no answer. He took his fist and banged loudly. A light came on, then the door opened slightly.

"I need to find Sanfia," Jakjak said, quietly.

A muscular man, looking to be about the same age as Jakjak, wiped his eyes and whispered, *"Ou konnen mwen pa kapab fè kado l' kache kote yo ye.* You know I can't give away her secret locations."

"Men, mwen pote fwape pa l '. Li gen medikal sekrè ki ap mete sou kote anpil moun. She has medical secrets that will save a lot of people."

"No, I can't."

"*An n pou nou bwè yon.'* Let's have a drink."

The reply was, "*Mwen pa t wiski nan yon semèn. Tonbe sou.* Come on in. I haven't had whiskey in over a week."

Jakjak motioned for me to stay in the van, and went inside.

I looked at my watch. 3:30 am.

Backstreets of Port au Prince
3:30 a.m.

I HAD TWO FRIENDS in Haiti, one was the surgeon, Tomas Duran, who lived in Leogane. It was three in morning, but I was desperate. I dialed his number. The phone rang on the other end. "He-ello ... " said a sleepy man.

"Tomas, good to hear your voice."

"Scott? Are you in Leogane? What time is it?"

"Tomas, I have to work fast. I think you know from the news that there was a bombing at my hospital. There may or may not be an Ebola epidemic that is about to start there as well."

"Yeah, I've been watching that on TV. So, how can I help?"

"We need to find Sanfia, the mambo, to get her zombie formula."

"What?"

"The zombie concoctions Sanfia used on me and Elizabeth Keyes probably caused us to have an immunity to Ebola."

"Wwwwwhat?"

"We can't be certain. But I think there was infected blood in the stuff that was given to me, because I'm immune. So is Keyes. The CDC is here with me and we need to locate Sanfia to get her zombie drugs. Keyes and I both had the zombie potions smeared into open wounds. Sanfia and her people knocked a gash into our heads with a rock and put some kind of mixture in. We're both immune. Do you know anybody who might know her?"

"Everybody knows of her. I know her."

"What interest do you have in the cult religions?"

"Scott, the 'cults,' as you call them, are a part of Haiti to which we all have exposure. But it is a supreme secret. People don't talk about it to outsiders. I know Sanfia and I have a lot of friends who are devoted followers of her."

It surprised me that a man of science such as Tomas was so familiar with the voodoo cult. "I'd appreciate any help from any source. The problem is, we need to work fast, before a lot of people in Jackson City get sick."

"How fast?"

I looked at my watch. It was 3:40 a.m. "I need to find her tonight."

"Sanfia disappeared," he said. "She hasn't gone to her religious meetings for weeks and nobody has seen her. But a small caravan of trucks drove through here a few weeks ago, about ten o'clock at night. People say it was Sanfia, leaving."

"Why do they say it was Sanfia?"

"Nobody saw Sanfia, but it was definitely her work crew. But let me explain something: Most of the zombies are used for slave labor. And the trucks were part of her

zombie following, her army. Another thing, they came at
night, and *nothing* gets done in Haiti after five o'clock in
the evening."

"That's two strikes against them."

"Maybe. But the third strike is there was a State Police
escort, *four cars*. That is a lot in Haiti. That has never
happened before. And they never turned on their sirens or
flashing lights. Our police here turn on sirens every time
they go for coffee, let alone an emergency."

"Where are they, in Leogane?"

"They passed through. One of my Dad's contacts said
they went from here to Dufort, and unloaded in Jacmel, by
the beach."

"Did they board ships?'

"No. No ships. There are no deep water docks near
the shore, just the fishing boats. Her workers all crowded
onto six boats. Nobody saw Sanfia, but people say that
they carried somebody or something wrapped in sheets to
a separate boat."

"Was that Sanfia?"

"That's a good guess."

"Did they say where they sailed?"

"It was dark, and the only information I have is that
they sailed south and hugged the coast."

Chapter 14

Backstreets of Port au Prince
4:00 a.m.

AS SOON AS I hung up, I started falling asleep. I tried to stay awake, but I couldn't.

Something suddenly shot me in the chest. I jumped, flailing my arms, then realized that is was the phone, set to vibrate.

It was Keyes.

She spoke quickly. "I can't locate Omar on the Internet, but I saw something on the news, on CNN and then on BBC. I'm almost certain that one of Farok's 747s landed in Adana, Turkey, three days ago, and loaded up a group of Syrian refugees."

"He's a wanted man. Why would he risk doing something public like that?"

"He wasn't public about it. The owner of that 747 is Kazakhstan West. I called Perkins and told him to look into it and he said it's a Kazakh West Airliner. Farok is mentioned nowhere."

"Then how do you know it's his plane? There are a lot of 747s flying in and out of Turkey."

"I know it's his plane. Even though it's marked as a Kazakhstan West airliner, there's one dead giveaway: His 747-8 is the only one with winglets, you know, the up-turned tips of a plane's wings? He had them added, to increase the lift in short runway situations."

"Are you sure? A lot of planes have those now."

"About ninety percent."

"In other words, there's a chance you're wrong?"

There was a pause before she said quietly, "Someday you'll learn to trust me. And that'll be your lucky day."

"But, Syrian refugees? I can't believe Omar Farok is in the humanitarian business. Where are they now?"

"Not in Kazakhstan, that's for sure. They're missing. They fell off the radar."

"What do you mean, 'fell off the radar?'"

"I mean it's still a big world out there and things still vanish. I tracked that plane's flight with ACARS, and apparently Farok's pilot switched off the primary ACARS, went to a second system, the Classic Aero, and then he dropped below 500 feet. So far no one's reported the arrival of the aircraft."

"That has Farok written all over it."

"That's what I said to Perkins. Scott, listen, that plane was headed west when it disappeared."

"What do you mean?"

"It took off from Turkey and didn't fly east, toward Kazakhstan. It flew west, out over the Atlantic."

"That's crazy."

"It got Perkins' attention, but only a little. He and the rest of them are treating it as a search-and-rescue case."

"Could it have gone all the way to Port au Prince?"

"I checked the flights into Port au Prince and no Kazakh 747 was listed. There's another 9500 foot strip in Les Cayes, 120 miles from Port au Prince. It's been under construction for two years and is partially completed, enough for one of Farok's daring pilots to attempt it. But like Port au Prince, there are no reports of a Kazakh plane landing there."

"Then, his 747 isn't in Haiti."

"I didn't say that."

It was not a pleasant thought for Elizabeth Keyes to be reminded of how well she knew Omar Farok's operations. She had been one of Farok's women. Keyes had worked on Farok's payroll as a courier first, and then later a slave. He'd made sure that she was indebted to him, squeezed, extorted from, terrorized.

"When I was with him, he landed his planes in a lot of countries with short airstrips that he lengthened by paying a work crew to level the space at either end. He'd pack and oil the ground to make the surface smooth enough so that his engines don't suck up dirt and gravel."

"So you think the plane landed at a clandestine airport."

"If anybody could pull off an operation like that, it would be Omar."

"How many Syrians boarded that plane?"

"From what I saw on the video clip, the refugees swarmed to get on, so I suppose the plane was loaded to the max."

"Which is how many?"

"A 747-8 can seat 467 with first, second, and third class passengers, 550 if it's only configured for business and 3rd class, and 605 if it's all third class seating. But if a jet like that traveled all the way from Turkey to Haiti, most of its fuel would be used up, greatly lightening the weight. That plane could have landed on an eight thousand foot runway. His pilots are accustomed to Omar's clandestine activities on short runways in third world countries."

"But could it take off in eight thousand feet?"

"With all those people off, the plane would be lighter. And burning most of its fuel in flight from Turkey? Another three hundred thousand pounds gone. Yes. He could leave with enough fuel to go to one of his 'secret hideaways' in the Caribbean for re-fueling."

I shook my head in amazement of Elizabeth. "Thanks for my math lesson. But what evil scheme does he have in mind for all those Syrians? "

"Don't know. I'll find his airport and *you* figure out the answer to that last question."

"Look at a map of Haiti and find where there is an attractive place near Leogane for him to set up operations."

"There are half a dozen cities on the Haitian coast."

I let out my breath. "You have to give me more than that. It's got to be some place where he could lengthen a runway and it wouldn't raise any eyebrows."

She studied the map again. "Wait. There's one island to the west, Ile a Vache, 6.5 miles off the coast of Les Cayes."

"Okay."

"It's a farming area, fifteen thousand people."

"Is there an airport?"

She scanned her computer before saying, "The list of airports in Haiti doesn't mention Ile a Vache, but searching under that name brings up a news article, saying the government is planning to make the island a major tourist attraction. It has a picture of hotel near an 'airport under construction.'"

Chapter 15

Backstreets of Port au Prince
4:15 a.m.

I WAS SOUND ASLEEP when a whistling Jakjak got in the car and drove away. I yawned and asked, "Why so happy?"

He laughed and slapped me on the thigh. "A stiff drink now and then ain't a bad thing. I know my people's reaction to alcohol."

"But you were supposed to make *him* drunk. You did it all backwards."

He laughed. "*O wi, Dokté.* But you ought ta see him. He drunk as a skunk, and never stopped talkin'. All I did was listen. An maybe drink. Just a little." He held out his hand toward me and parted his index finger an inch above his thumb.

I smelled the air and added, "You're about six inches off your whiskey measurement, Jacques Jacobo, and schnockered."

He laughed. "But Lord, after the third drink, he give me more answers than I had questions."

"Tell me everything."

He stopped the van and turned to me. "Sanfia's done gone from here. She taken all her zombies, an' potions, an fish an toad frog skins, an parts of dead bodies, and she has leff."

"Why did she leave?"

"She didn't do it of her own choosin'. They make her go. She wouldn't leave all her people, not for anything."

"Not even for money?"

"She like her money. But she like all her followers even more. No. Money does lots of things, but money not come between her and her people."

"What do we do now?"

"De ees one more place she kepp her zombies. We go there. He say dat de are still some of Sanfia's people here. But he say de are en a very dangerous place."

Chapter 16

Backstreets of Port au Prince
4:35 a.m.

JAKJAK DROVE DOWN THE backstreets for fifteen minutes before parking in front of a graveyard. We both had the military-issue flashlights that the CDC had given us, but we didn't want to turn them on, even though it was pitch black.

With the lights off, I held Jakjak's shirt as he walked through a wooded area in the cemetery. We were on a crudely cleared foot path. I was breathing heavily. We were walking toward a crumbling house with a collapsed roof. I lit my flashlight from time to time. I had no idea where we were and stayed on Jakjak's heels to keep from stumbling on the grave stones. We passed through a wrought iron gate, and then I snapped the light on to see rib bones, from either a large animal, or a human. I looked ahead to see the silhouette of Jakjak standing at another badly twisted wrought iron gate, farther on, and knew I'd lost him, and ran to catch up. I started to move and stumbled on a concrete pad sticking up from the ground. There was a five-foot-high cement cross there with burn marks all over it: Vodoun sacrifice altar.

When we reached the damaged house, we went through a break in the fence and walked around for a moment before finding the basement door. He knocked three times. After no response, he turned the door handle, then shouldered the door, forcing it open.

We turned on the flashlights and explored. Flies circled a dried puddle of blood on the floor. There were blood stains on the army cot beside it.

Jakjak looked around. "De nobody been here for weeks. The food's all gone and the place is filthy. Sanfia would have cleaned this place every day."

Jakjak shook his head as he said, "I hope she let go de spirits she captured in the *tri-bon-age*. Maybe the spirits go back and the zombies be real people again."

"You don't believe all that, do you?"

He thought for a moment. "Yes, *Dokte*. And you seen the zombies. That part of what Sanfia did ees true."

There was another door. Jakjak cracked it open and looked in with his flashlight. The odor of death hit us in the face. We stepped inside and he closed the door behind me. There were three folding chairs in the room that were broken apart. Deep holes had been knocked in the sheetrock walls.

Jakjak turned to me. "One of de zombies smashed de chairs against the walls. Sanfia never allow that."

I followed him through an open arch to another room. The stench was stronger. He opened another closed door and we saw the source of the smell: There were six bodies scattered on the floor. I put my forearm over my nose to block the odor. The arms were torn from two bodies and the flesh had been ripped from the bones.

Jakjak turned to me. "These are Sanfia's zombies. It looks like de was locked in here and some of them starved to death."

"But the torn off arms..."

"Some of them lived and ate parts of the others."

My stomach turned.

A shadow moved. I turned. Jakjak shouted, "Look out!"

A frail man swung part of an arm at me. I ducked and raised my fist to hit the guy, but Jakjak called out, "Don't hit him. He too weak. Just back off."

The man was growling, like an animal, as Jakjak stepped between us.

The spectacle of this man, a zombie, was almost too much to bear. He looked like a man possessed. He swung the bloody arm around in the room of death and growled, a pathetic, macabre shell of a human being, zombie-fide, wrecked, a million miles from his real life, and living now in the dark.

Jakjak spoke in a soft voice, "*Sa se byen pase. Sa se byen pase. Nou se zanmi yon Sanfia. Nou ap ede ou. Nou ap ede ou ou*. It's alright. It's alright. We are friends of Sanfia. We'll help you. We'll help you."

The skinny man's voice was shrill. *"Nou tout ki grangou. Pa gen moun vin jwenn nou. Ki kote Sanfia ale?* We all hungry. Nobody come to us. Where Sanfia go?"

Jakjak reached to take the arm from the man and he snatched it from Jakjak's grip and swung it at him. Jakjak stepped back and repeated quietly, *"Sa se byen pase. Sa se byen pase."*

The man whined like an animal as Jakjak spoke softly. The man listened for a few minutes as Jakjak inched closer to him and put his arm around his shoulder. He didn't move for a minute, then jumped away. Jakjak spoke some more. The man was mesmerized by the quiet words and finally dropped the arm and walked to Jakjak's side.

I backed away as Jakjak cradled him in his arms like a mother would a baby. He kept talking softly and eventually the man began to speak. After what seemed like half an hour, Jakjak turned to me. "His name is Bartholome. He's the only one left alive. They've had no food since Sanfia left several weeks ago. He lived by eating the meat of his zombie friends. Sanfia keeps bottled water in a closet in the next room."

We went to the other room. Jakjak led Bartholome to the door and said, "Drink."

Bartholome went to a dining room chair, sat, and folded his hands.

I was in awe. I began to speak quietly to the man and his eyes glazed over. "He must understand English," I said.

"No, not this man. But lots of Sanfia's zombies talk English. He don't know what you say, but he charmed by your attitude and quite voice, like Sanfia."

Jakjak opened several bottles of water and placed them on the table.

"What's the plan now?" asked Jakjak.

"We have to call Reed. He'll take care of Bartholome. This zombie probably has the same immunity to Ebola as Elizabeth and I do. They can take him and analyze his blood. If he has immunity, they can use his immune serum back at the quarantine."

Chapter 17

Backstreets of Port au Prince
4:55 a.m.

I HEARD THE PHONE ring on the other end of the line, and then when Reed answered, I said, "Reed, I've found a zombie."

"Dr. James? What the ... " Reed said. "The police are pissed, Scott. Seriously. You should of just told me that you were going to break out. I would have helped you. I'm on your side, Scott. And I don't think you're a terrorist or anything else. I believe your story."

"Thanks, Andy. I need a friend right now."

"No kidding."

"Do you know where I am?"

"Yes, I do. The entire United States intelligence

apparatus knows where you are. That little 'pill,' as Perkins calls it, works."

"Okay, then come out here in one of the helicopters. To hell with what Perkins said. We have to do this quickly. You're going to have to come and get this guy and take him back for testing. How's your French?"

"It's passable."

"Okay. Listen: He's a zombie, with the mind of a child. If you are belligerent, he'll fight you 'til he dies. Talk to him quietly, like you would a very young child. Treat him gently and tell him that you are a friend of Sanfia and he'll cooperate."

"I can do that. I've never talked to a zombie before, but I'm good at sweet talking my kids into doing things they don't want to do."

Jakjak took the phone and gave Reed the specifics of our location.

Chapter 18

Day 3
Somewhere in Haiti
Sunrise

IT WAS DAYLIGHT NOW. The helicopter looked like a giant beacon for anyone to see, anyone who wanted to locate us.

The noise and downdraft was intense. The big machine's wind was so concentrated that you felt like you might lose your footing at any moment. Jakjak stood there with his legs spread, braced against Bartholome, holding the zombie upright.

The chopper touched down and Reed jumped out. The zombie raised his fist to strike Reed as he approached, but Jakjak crooned, "Bartholome. Bartholome."

Reed, when he got close, grasped Bartholome's face in his hands and whispered into the poor man's ear. In broken French, he said, "I am a friend of Sanfia. She told me to come and rescue you."

Bartholome cocked his head and looked at Reed.

"Yes," Reed said, gently. "Sanfia loves you."

The zombie answered, "Sanfia?"

"Bartholome, Sanfia wants me to take you to the hospital, to care for you."

Reed put his arm around the confused man and began to lead him to the helicopter. Sarge stepped down and put a blanket around the bewildered man's shoulders.

After he'd got Bartholome aboard, Reed turned and looked at me and shouted over the rotor noise, "Jesus, Scott! He's malnourished! He's barely alive! Don't the drugs wear off?"

"Maybe they do, maybe they don't. I suppose they do, but these guys have been put through God only knows what. I've seen this before. Some don't ever really recover. Who knows what's been done to them?"

Suddenly we heard sirens. Police vehicles, coming from behind.

"Sounds like they're coming here," I said. "They followed the helicopter."

"No shit. After your little stunt back at the staging area, everybody's watching us. You guys have to come back on the chopper."

"No! We have to locate Sanfia!"

"They're going to arrest you two and put you *under* the jail, Scott. And Perkins is losing patience. So I don't know if you can be assured that he'll get you out."

"No! We have to stay free! They'll only get us if they

catch us." I looked at Roberts. "Take off!" I yelled. "Take off! GO!"

I pushed Reed aboard and the chopper started lifting off. I looked at Jakjak and said, "Get us to one of Sanfia's caves, or something. We can't work with police around."

I followed Jakjak, who ran between a row of houses, across a ravine too deep for the patrol cars to pass, and to a hillside with thick underbrush. After going a hundred yards from the road, Jakjak squatted. "I been to this very spot when I ran from the police when I was a kid."

We sat quietly for fifteen minutes.

I was beginning to feel safe when suddenly they were behind us. We turned to see the gleam of guns pointed at us, guns from a dozen cops. We had no choice but to raise our hands and stand.

Chapter 19

Somewhere in Haiti
Time unknown

JAKJAK AND I WERE handcuffed and taken to a police van at the roadside. I looked at our ten captors. Two wore police uniforms and the rest were dressed in cleaned and pleated jeans and colorful sport shirts that were starched and pressed. All were youthful, between twenty and twenty-five years-old, and fit. Neither Jakjak nor I recognized any of them. They emptied my pockets and took my phone.

One of the men, a man with a heavily pocked face grabbed my hair in his fist and thrust a short, thick-bladed knife to my throat. "Doctor James, I am the one who will take your life, like this." He jerked his arm and made a quick movement with the knife, slicing my throat over my trachea. I felt the pain of the sharp knife, and then the blood, flowing down my neck. He did it so fast, it took my breath away. I struggled against the strong arms of those who held me, waiting for the death blow and my decapitation. But he laughed and turned to Jakjak. "That is but a preview of the death that will come to you and your doctor friend. But I will do it slow, so you will feel every movement of the knife, every pain that your body can sense, and all the horror that death can have." He glared at Jakjak and then laughed again before walking away. I put my chin on my chest to compress the neck wound and try to stop the blood flow.

They placed a black sack over Jakjak's head and threw him in the van. Two guys stretched out a thick blanket made of a flexible, metallic fabric, rolled me up it, and shoved me in the van beside Jakjak.

I could hear Jakjak's muffled voice through my thick covering, "*Dokte*, why they do us different?"

"Beats me. Did you recognize any of them?"

"No. But they are not Haitians. They speak some African language, all 'cept the guy with the knife. He only talks English, not good English like you and me, but like someone from England."

Despite our dire circumstance, I found humor in Jakjak's words. He was well educated, with a college degree from a well respected school, the University d'Etat d'Haiti, and admired in his country for his command of the English language. I like self confidence in an individual. He was proud of himself, but not as proud as *I* was of him. And proud to be his friend.

Soon we heard the sounds of a jet engine and knew that we must be at an airport. They pulled us from their van and threw us in what seemed to be a baggage compartment. We had no idea where we were or where we were going.

Chapter 20

Temporary Headquarters of the CDC Team
8:00 a.m.

REED'S PHONE RANG. IT was Dr. Wilson, calling from the quarantine. "Dr. Reed, or can I call you Andy?"

"I like Andy, thanks. Are there any 'sickies' in the quarantine group?"

"Not a one. Tape thermometers are on the foreheads of all of them and there are no elevated temperatures or any of the symptoms of Ebola."

"That's good. The longer they stay free of symptoms, the longer we have to find the cure. I'm hoping it's the Zaire strain. That takes the longest to incubate, and in theory, so long as they are treated before the fever begins, they are curable."

"I appreciate your optimism. I hope you're right. How about my buddy, Scott James? Is he staying out of your hair?"

"He helped me get a live zombie. We're busy testing these new specimens for immunity."

"Tell him hello, and that I'm real sorry about his situation with the Mayor."

"He'll appreciate that, but I haven't heard from him in two hours."

"Is he out bar hopping?"

"I certainly hope so. He's running around the streets of Haiti, and I have been calling him for an hour and he won't answer."

"Uh oh," Dr. Wilson said. "I hope Jakjak's with him. He knows Haiti."

Chapter 21

Somewhere in Haiti
8:00 a.m.

THE FLIGHT TOOK ABOUT twenty minutes. They threw us in the back of an open bedded truck and drove less than five minutes before we stopped and heard the opening of a rusty gate. The truck proceeded down what was obviously a muddy, uneven road, then stopped again.

Two men carried me as Jakjak walked. We went down several flights of stairs and then walked down a long hallway. After traveling for what seemed like about one hundred yards, we turned and walked down another hallway.

At the end, they opened up a room and put me down on the floor. They unwrapped me and took off the handcuffs, then left, bolting the door from the outside. The room was about the size of something you might see at motel, and empty, save for a large mattress on the floor, a corner commode, and a tiny sink.

"Any guess where we are?"

"Well, *Dokte*, we didn't go far from Port au Prince, we near the ocean, and that was the roughest plane landing I ever had."

"I agree with the rough landing. It seemed like we landed on a soft, mushy surface, bounced on a smooth hard surface, then bounced again onto a second hard surface, with gravel or something that made the wheels whine."

"Yeah, like the runway was three pieces of different pavement, pieced together."

"Why do you think we're near the ocean?"

"*Dokte*, didn't you smell the salt air when we got out of the plane?"

"Why, no. All I smelled was the musty vegetation when we left the road, like we were in the countryside." I took a deep breath. "The section we're in has been newly constructed. Can't you tell by the smell?"

He took a breath and nodded. "Yes. I smelled the same 'new' as we first entered the building."

"Look at the room we're in. It's just been built. So, we're in a coastal area, with a rough landing strip, in the sub-basement of a new building. We can't call Reed and tell them we've been kidnapped, and our GPS trackers can't be picked up down here."

"*Dokte*, de blanket de put on you was Mylar or maybe some kind of metal. I think when de do dat, you signal goes dark. But maybe mine was still working. De put just a regular blanket on me."

Chapter 22

General Perkins' Temporary Offices
Homestead Air Base
9:00 a.m.

"JAMES AND THE OTHER guy are gone," Lt. Moss said in her husky voice. "The signal stopped and didn't come back."

"What?" Perkins said. "Get Reed on the phone, asap."

Perkins' temporary suite at Homestead was nice. He had Lt. Moss set up in the other room, a spacious conference room, and right behind his office, a small but comfortable sleeping quarters. The phone next to his computer rung. He picked it up and said, "Where the hell is Scott James?"

"General Perkins, we're having some degree of difficulty here. The Haitian Police are around us like flies. Everywhere we go, a group of them circle and follow us."

The General "ahemed" and asked, "Why is that such a bother? The President promised his support. The police he delegated to you shows his commitment to that promise."

"But the police are a total nuisance. They swarm us every time we go out to interview people. And Dr. James has disappeared because of this. He and Jakjak went alone to find Sanfia. To get her, he had to go without the police."

"Didn't he use the police escort?"

"Well, no."

"So, he's out roaming around the streets of Haiti alone?"

"Jakjak was with him. He knows Port au Prince and the people very well."

"But, you're saying: He's dicking around Haiti without the police escort I planned for you all?"

"Well, yes."

"Ahem. But he didn't follow my directive, now did he?"

"No, but he was justified in his actions because—"

"Listen, doctor. I've had a long conversation with the President of Haiti. Do you know what a pain in the ass Scott James was on his prior trip to Haiti?"

"Why, no."

"You know, they don't want him back in Haiti because of all the trouble he stirred up on his last visit there. And he was back in the States for less than six months before he screwed up so badly they kicked him out of his own hometown. And they don't want him back!"

"General, do you realize we're on the brink of a major epidemic of Ebola in North Carolina? And that we must find Sanfia, if she even exists, or we have no access to whatever it was that made Scott James immune?"

"You goddamn doctors have your heads up your asses, thinking you are your own bosses."

Chapter 23

Temporary CDC Center
9:15 a.m.

REED HAD JUST GOTTEN off the call from General Perkins informing him that Scott James' GPS signal was gone when his phone rang yet again. It wasn't Perkins. It was a number he didn't recognize. "This is Dr. Reed," he said.

"Dr. Reed, this is Elizabeth Keyes. I can't seem to get Dr. James on his phone."

Reed informed her that James had been last seen running from the police, and now his GPS tracker was no longer signaling.

"Dr. Reed, I have an idea of where Dr James could be. There is an island off the coast of Haiti called Ile-à-Vache. It was a quiet farming community until Haiti decided to develop it into a tourist resort. A twenty acre parcel was given to a Kazakhstani National, Sattar Aslanov, in return for his building a luxury hotel that would accommodate five hundred guests. The project was completed about three weeks ago. The hotel has been finished for three weeks but there haven't been any guests checked in. A wealthy man like Aslanov didn't get rich by letting any of his properties remain unused for nearly a month."

"Okay, but what does any of this mean to us?"

"There was a report of a Kazakhstan West 747 leaving Adana, Turkey, three days ago, loaded with Syrian refugees. That plane never arrived in Kazakhstan, but I've been tracking it based on its last known position and I think I know where it might have gone. The jet was heading in the direction of Haiti's airspace the night it left Syria. I'm almost certain that this is Omar Farok's plane, with the Kazakh West logo painted on it."

"Uh...I'm new to this game. How do you know that it's owned by terrorists?"

"Because Farok has modified his jets so that they can land on very short runways."

"Are you sure about that?"

Keyes let out a long sigh. "No. I'm not sure. But that jet didn't land anywhere else. Ile-à-Vache, 'Cow Island,' has a 3000-foot runway that's been recently lengthened by 3500 feet."

"A 747 needs a lot more real estate. Even I know that."

"It does, for commercial pilots with paying customers who sue when even small things go wrong. With his modified jets, Omar's pilots are capable of landing within eight thousand feet, maybe a lot less, and nobody sues him for spilling hot coffee on their laps because of rough landings. His pilots don't mind landing on rough surfaces, I assure you, like recently bull dozed, raw land, or in cattle fields with metal strips, you know, the Matson Matting, like the military uses. I saw him do it once in Kenya."

"What does Perkins think about all this?"

"He thinks I have a wild imagination."

"I'm new to this game, Ms. Keyes. I'll have to get back to you."

Chapter 24

Sub-basement Jail
Location Unknown
Time Unknown

FOUR GUARDS, DRESSED IN their starched, colorful sports shirts and trousers, opened our cell, and then escorted us down the long corridor to a new room.

We sat at the back of an assembly room that was filled with twenty chairs facing a sixty-inch TV. We were securely chained to our seats and surrounded by guards who kept their guns pointed at our faces.

The wait was brief. Six more men, casually dressed in sporty outfits matching the four guards with us, escorted a man who was dressed in a distinguished looking tuxedo. He had a small, thin face, and a thin mustache above his narrow lips. He looked about five-foot-eight, but had two-inch elevator shoes on his small feet.

I didn't recognize him until he spoke. His fake bass tone and careful enunciation of each word gave him away.

Omar Farok. The worst one of them all. A mutant strain. And the least-known, outside the intelligence community. Omar was an outcast who wanted to rule the world. A man so nasty and vile I could barely look at him. Even some of the other terrorists had disowned him. Vaguely royal, he claimed to be a Prince from the Sudan, with oil money and a fleet of jets.

"Is this the real Omar Farok, or just some short ugly guy with a glued on nose."

He glared at me for a second and then looked away at his accomplices. "If they try to escape, shoot them in their legs. I'm not ready for them to die yet."

He turned and looked at me with fire in his eyes. "Yes. I am God's voice to all my people. Sometimes I have to be His military leader, and days like today, I am His diplomatic emissary to the people of Syria."

"Syria?" I asked. I thought of his 747 that took on the refugees in Adana, Turkey. "So, this is the place you brought those 467 refugees from Adana?"

His face turned red. "That's all the seats I had but they kept piling in. We have 490. And I am always amazed at the skills of your girlfriend in learning that information. It's a pity that she couldn't make it to the party."

"And I congratulate the pilot that landed on the miniature runway here on Ile a Vache."

His mouth dropped open and for a second, he looked at me with his eyes opened widely.

For a brief second, I was happy. With Elizabeth's information, my rough plane landing, and Farok's inability to control his emotional facial expressions, I knew where I was. I had to either escape or in some way make my location known to Perkins and Reed.

He walked over to me and rubbed the wound on my throat. I let him have his fun as he wiped away the scab and watched my blood ooze out. "You have much to look forward to. I want you to live just long enough to see the death of your most respected leaders. The only thing I regret is that my queen, Elizabeth, isn't here. Well, I'll swing by America and pick her up. She makes a good slave. A slave queen. Brilliant, isn't it, Dr. James?"

I felt blood running on my chest and put my chin down to stop it. Leaning awkwardly back in my chair, I looked him in the eye. "I'd applaud you if you'd get rid of some of the 'respected leaders' in Jackson City."

His head dropped backwards as he laughed as hard as he was capable. "Yes, you have been humiliated by all of your hometown peers. I did that to you. You are a man on the run, a man without a country. You have no friends. They will all salute me when I broadcast your beheading on world wide television. Everyone will be happy you're dead. And what do I have to make this even worse for you? It will actually be a double header. I'll kill your President, which you will witness on this jumbo sized TV."

Farok turned on his heel and walked away.

"What about Jakjak?" I called out. "Are you going to release him?"

He stopped and turned around to look at Jakjak. "You will face the ultimate horror. You will be made into a zombie."

Then he left.

We were unshackled by the guards and taken back to our cell. Jakjak looked pale as they slammed the door. He started to cry.

"Jakjak, snap out of it. Nobody'll make you a zombie. We must either escape or make sure that Perkins and Reed can find us."

Jakjak was a big, strong man, physically, but he was still mentally subservient to his deeply ingrained voodoo beliefs, and understandably terrified of becoming a zombie. "I rather have my head cut than be zombie."

"They're not doing either to you. Now let's talk it out."

He wiped his eyes. "Jes tell me what to do."

"We have these GPS trackers in our bodies. They're keeping us here in the sub-basement so our signal isn't getting out. All we have to do is get one floor up, maybe two, and they'll pick up the signal."

Chapter 25

Temporary CDC Center
10:30 a.m.

"REED?" WILSON SAID OVER the phone, "We definitely have three patients here with fevers."

"Really? That would be very fast. That can't be right. Usually you don't see symptoms of Ebola for about eight days. Are you sure?"

"Well, we're sure of the fevers, but we're just now looking at these people's lab work. But it's strange. None of these people were near the blast, and I don't believe the virus could've gotten inside breaks in their skin."

"Are they cut up? Do they have lacerations?"

"Yes, but they were a long way away from the ER. It could be something else, not Ebola. What's your status?"

"We don't know where Scott James is right now. Or Jakjak. We should have the test results from our zombie within the hour. Have you been able to get any drugs for your people?"

"No, I haven't. I have to say, people have been very tight-lipped about this. It's hard to get any kind of commitment from anyone. I've talked to a lot of doctors by phone and they aren't helpful. It's crazy. And the clock is definitely ticking. If we get a full blown outbreak here, it's going to be bad."

Chapter 26

Somewhere on Ile-à-Vache
11:30 a.m.

FOUR GUARDS CAME AND escorted us down the long hallway. We went through a door and proceeded down a second hallway, which, like the one where our cell was, had a floor and walls of rough concrete. None of the guards understood English. They spoke in an Arabic language. We passed more doorways and we could hear mumblings and groaning from the occupants inside.

"Zombies?" I whispered to Jakjak.

He looked straight ahead and quickly barked, "*Kote manman ou yeis*. Is your Mama there?"

I heard someone scratching and a voice asking about Sanfia.

The guards turned and looked at Jakjak, but said nothing.

"What did they say?" I whispered.

"Mama Sanfia, why did you leave us? You talk to us through the door but never come in. Don't you love us?"

"So, she's here somewhere."

He nodded.

The rough hallway led us to an elevator that took us from the sub-basement to the basement. The doors opened to a hall with a thick piled carpet covering the floor, and smooth, pastel-painted walls. Along the top we could see an exquisitely carved crown molding. I inhaled deeply. The sweet fragrance of the space we entered contrasted sharply with the musty, stale air of our jail cell.

They led us into a large banquet hall, beautifully adorned with a rich carpet and floral patterned wallpaper. The huge room dwarfed the table for twelve in its center. A dozen of the brightly dressed guards with Kalashnikov rifles stood stiffly around the walls.

Then, Farok made his grand entrance. His soldiers applauded. A short, frail, elderly woman followed him, and sat beside him at the end of the table, opposite us. It was Sanfia.

Sanfia was a legend and a specter, a person with an alarming face and aura. Her thin cotton dress was stark white and adorned with intricate lace that clashed with her deep, drawn cheeks and lips. Stark white powder lay pancaked on her face, giving her a distinctly dead look. She, in fact, rarely appeared without ritual paint on her face. As a Vodoun priestess, she had made a small fortune using zombies as slave labor. The drugged men and women were used as work gangs for government projects.

Sanfia's prestige was always enough to win one contract after another, and her zombie-fide work gangs could be seen throughout Haiti, working on the roads and sewers. At night, they were frequently paraded on the Sanpwel stage, lit by wild flashing lights.

Sanfia sat perfectly still and very somber-like, regal, looking stiffly ahead, and never our way.

Farok identified her as the "Impératice Angelina Sanfina, the grand Hounfor of Haiti."

She bowed her head only slightly.

He pointed at us. "And you, Impératice, do you know these men?"

Without looking at us she bowed her head slightly.

"I want these men to be witnesses to your accomplishments in making zombies that obey my every command."

She made no indication that she heard these words.

The servers came and poured Araq for the four of us. I took a sip, but it tasted foul. I looked at Jakjak and shook my head. He got my message as he held the beverage to his lips but never put it in his mouth.

They first served tabbouleh, a parsley and tomato salad. "The finest of Syrian cuisine," Farok announced.

It was Jakjak this time who shook his head as I lifted a fork full to my lips.

The second course was muqlubbeh, rice topped with eggplant, and rare beefsteak. It looked good. Jakjak cut a piece and had it in his mouth when Sanfia, very slightly, shook her head, 'No.'

We both pretended to eat, but our host saw our ploy. "I have the best food money can buy and you refuse to eat."

He put his hands on his hips and screamed, "Now EAT!"

I put my napkin on my plate. "I've been very ill since I passed a large bug, probably a parasite of some nature. I just can't eat a thing."

I saw a very faint smile cross his face. "Very humorous, Dr. James, as usual. Well, I sincerely hope you feel better. And you, Jakjak?"

"I'm very well, but I am from Haiti and don't eat this kind of food. Sanfia says it ees bad."

He looked at Sanfia. "Is that true, Impératice?"

She didn't answer.

"Since I am the only person who is hungry," Farok said very politely, "you all can watch me eat."

Now was the time to work on him. I said, "So tell me, Omar ... "

"Don't call me Omar!"

"Sorry, Omar. Eh ... Great Emir."

Farok took a deep breath and blew it out slowly, "Call me President of ISIS. I am a great and powerful man, chosen by Allah to be the supreme leader of ..." He paused before continuing, "not just Syria, but the World."

I felt my face turn red. Then I put on my 'stupid face' and said, "Gee, you're really not a world leader type at all. I mean, didn't ISIS say 'No' to you?"

"Quite amusing, Dr. James. You should be glad that my guards don't understand English, otherwise they'd cut out your tongue."

"You tell people that a special place in Heaven awaits them when they die. You reject knowledge and wish to put the world back into the ignorance of the 5th Century. You just want chaos to stop the world so that everyone will look at you."

Farok's frown deepened and his face turned red. Then he took a deep breath and gave a half hearted laugh. "No. God sent me here to kill everyone who doesn't believe, people just like you. And that is my mission."

"And you believe you must get rid of all religions except yours?

"I believe in strict interpretation of the Koran."

"You hide behind your own interpretation. But a religion as great as Islam and a prophet as good as Mohammad could not possibly be so backward. Even others of your own religion have turned away from you. But they don't dare speak out for fear of some brainwashed nut killing them."

Farok threw down his fork and glared.

"Maybe it's not your teaching that radicalizes your recruits, but their addiction to the 'Middle East speed' you give them, Captagon. Does it really make them bullet proof, like you tell them?"

He stood and stared at me for what seemed a long time. "Enough of this charade, Omar. Why are we here and what are you doing with all the refugees from Syria?"

"I cannot understand why Elizabeth has chosen you over me."

I shrugged. "She was looking for a man."

"That bitch. If she hadn't rejected my authority, she'd be here beside me. She'd be dressed in the finest designer dresses from France instead of those dime store rags you wear. And her hand would have to struggle to lift the heavy diamond I offered her back in Yemen."

He continued to eat in silence, but I knew I had made him mad, so I continued. "Omar, eh, Great Emir, you have Sanfia's zombies here. What are you going to use them for?"

Still, he was quiet.

"Are they here for your executioners to practice on before they start on me, Jakjak, and Sanfia?"

I watched Sanfia's reaction as she looked harshly at Farok.

"All your money cannot buy her cooperation," I said, knowing I was on to something, "knowing that you are basically an evil man. A man who not only kills and tortures his enemies, but also his friends." I turned to Sanfia. "This man uses his wealth to buy people and soldiers to do his evil bidding."

He stood and screamed, "Let her go with the wind! I brought her zombies here to help me, but I now can make my own zombies! And I will slaughter them all, along with Sanfia, before I leave this island! I have no need for any of you!" He threw his plate at me, then took a rifle from one of his guards, and rushed at me. He swung the butt of the gun at me but I ducked, and then stood. I glanced around the room to see every rifle in the place aimed at me. I'd gone too far with Farok and I knew it. I raised my hands and said, "I'm very sorry to be so rude. I'm sorry Great Emir," I said, making a deep bow, "Forgive me."

He swung his tiny fist and hit my neck. It had no force, but it did knock the scab from my neck. As blood flowed, the guards smiled. Farok smiled, too, as he saw their reaction and hit me again. He wiped the blood from his hand with my dinner napkin and returned to his place at the table.

"I brought Sanfia's zombies here to help me, but I now can make my own zombies. I can also give anyone I want amnesia, which is a powerful tool, I assure you. I no longer need her services. She will suffer the same fate as you."

For the first time, Sanfia looked fearful. Obviously, she didn't know. I knew I'd just made an important ally.

Farok growled, as fearsome as he could, and screamed at us: "You berate me before the God that gave me the power to deliver this world back to Him! I will kill all that do not bow to me and the great Allah. You will see my great leadership in two days." He shook his finger at me and continued, "You will see all this before you die!"

Tears started to roll down Sanfia's face. It was the first time I'd ever seen the powerful woman show any signs of being human.

"Throw them all in the same room!" Farok yelled, "I need her no more!" He then stormed out of the room.

In the sudden vacuum of Omar's departure, Jakjak got up and walked hurriedly over to Sanfia, which drew the guards.

I saw my chance.

I bolted from my chair to the nearest door. A guard raised his gun to shoot me, but another called out to him and he held his fire. I ran down a short hallway and then bounded up a flight of stairs in three giant steps, as the guards chased me. I threw open the door at the top of the stairs and was astounded at what I saw.

I was in a modern hotel, with a huge lobby, with all the doormen, waiters, and servicemen wearing the same brightly colored casual dress as Farok's guards. The ceiling was high, with balconies on each of the eight floors that overlooked the main area.

Even stranger, there were fifty or so guests wandering around in the lobby, all looking half-asleep. They weren't zombies exactly, but very close, definitely drugged, and unaware of their surroundings.

In the crowd, I briefly saw a face that I knew. I made eye contact. The tall, muscular, African-American man's eyes bulged, and his chin receded the moment he saw me. Then he turned his face away quickly. It was Emmanuel, Sanfia's right hand man.

"Emmanuel! Help me! Help me!"

My pursuers gang tackled me and I fell hard on the floor. "Emmanuel! They're going to kill you and Sanfia! Farok's going to kill everybody! You have to alert the authorities!"

Emmanuel, who was dressed in a dark suit, seemed, vaguely, to be in charge of the half-sleeping quests wandering around. He shouted at the guards, "What is this man doing here? What is this?" His words were in English and went unanswered. But clearly he was in charge, because he started rounding up the semi-zombies.

I now had four strong guards holding my arms back. "Emmanuel! You're in danger! Sanfia's going to be killed! You will be, too!"

The last I saw of him was the back of his blue suit. He was gently herding the guests into a corner.

I was hauled back to the cell in the sub basement, where Jakjak and Sanfia awaited me.

The guard threw me hard on the floor and then slammed the door behind him.

Chapter 27

General Perkins' Temporary Offices
Homestead Air Base
Noon

Dr. James' GPS blipped. Lt. Moss was watching. Her eyes popped open. She scanned a map of Haiti, then walked into Perkins' office. "I have Dr. James' signal. It's coming from Ile-à-Vache, Cow Island."

"Where the hell is that?"

She showed him the map of Haiti. "A small island, roughly eight kilometers off the coast of Haiti."

"How far from the CDC people?"

"About 120 kilometers."

"Why would he be there?"

"Don't know. The signal from the tracker was there for a minute, then it disappeared."

"What do you mean, disappeared?"

"The GPS pill was either destroyed, placed in a metal container, or taken to a place where the satellite can't see it, a basement room or something. But it was there for just a moment. I saw it."

"Keep an eye on that thing. I'll call Reed."

Reed picked up on the first ring.

"Dr. Reed? He's on Ile-a-Vache, seven miles off the coast, or at least his signal is."

"What are his coordinates?"

While Reed wrote down the latitude and longitude of Dr. James' last known position, Perkins said, "It looks like he's either in a hotel that's being built over there, or near it. What's he doing over there, Reed?"

"I would imagine he's tracking down Sanfia or he's been taken by the police over there."

"Taken by the police? What does that mean?"

"I mean that the situation isn't 'a little hot' here General, it's *damned* hot. I think he's been kidnapped."

"Oh my God. What is it with you people? Can't you stay out of trouble? I suppose the next thing you're going to say is that you want my permission to take the security detail to that island to locate him?"

"Yes. That's exactly what I want to do. He's probably in trouble."

Perkins took a deep breath and blew into the phone, "That is not the way to handle it. I'm not going to cause trouble with the locals just to go out in search of that goddamn doctor! Let him rot on that island!"

The General mumbled under his breath.

"The CDC has close contact with the US Secretary of State," Reed finally said. "If you don't authorize my request, I'll be obligated to go over your head. We have to finish this mission."

"Okay. Just hang on. I'll look into it."

Chapter 28

Sub-basement Jail
12:05 p.m.

JAKJAK HELD THE CRYING Sanfia in his arms ten minutes before she spoke.

"Farok is truly evil. My biggest mistake in life was to take his money. He has taken all my children."

I asked, "Do you mean your zombies?"

"Yes. They are my only children. I made them and I must care for them, all one hundred. With all the money Farok gave me, I can take care of them for many, many years without them having to repair roads and dig ditches for Haiti." She turned and pointed to me. "You are a good man. You talk truth."

Jakjak interrupted. "Sanfia, tell him how you get all your powers. Dr. James think you no different than anyone else."

I raised my brow. He was right about his statement, but he said it like he still believed in her. I listened quietly.

"I am clairvoyant. It's a trait inherited by only a fraction of my people, no more that once in a generation. I have that trait, as did my grandmother, who took me as her child when this gift was first discovered. She nurtured my abilities, and taught me how to use them. I was able to predict future happenings. All around me were in awe of this. My grandmother was also named Angelique Sanfina, like me, and they called her Sanfia, just as they call me. She taught me how to render justice to my people that was fair and decide who in our society were guilty and when to issue the punishment of zombie rendering. And I learned from her not only drugs to make zombies, but also medicinal plants that I have used over my years to cure people. I cured Jakjak when he almost died in the prison beneath Haiti's National Palace."

"What plants did you use to cure Jakjak?"

"Oh, I used no plants on him at all. I used IV Rocephin and plasmanate, and I gave him IM Demerol for his pain."

"Rocephin? Demerol? Plasmanate? Only a medical doctor can administer those."

"I am well-versed in western medicine, as it is called. I had plenty of time to study while Baby Doc had me imprisoned. A doctor brought me all his medical books, and still provides me with his journals."

"How did you get the drugs? No matter how much

medicine you know, you have to have a medical license to prescribe drugs."

"There are many pharmacists in my Sanpwel."

"How did you escape death from the firing squad when Baby Doc was president?"

"During my six years in prison beneath the National Palace, I treated not only the infirmities of those imprisoned with me but also the soldiers who had rotating duties in guarding us. I treated them and their families and cured them when their western trained physicians could not. Even in prison, I remained the spiritual leader of the people of Port au Prince. I found passages of tunnels to escape for my Sanpwel meetings and the guards never reported me. In fact, they all attended the meetings. And when the President ordered my execution, they burned my chest with a cigarette to make it look like a bullet hole. I fell down when they intentionally fired over my head. After they made my "death photograph" which you obviously saw, the guards set me free. The prison tunnels became my home for more than fifteen years until the politics changed. When I emerged to the outside world, many people thought I'd risen from the dead, like Jesus Christ. Whether I did good or bad by it, I didn't correct them. They gave me great respect, but I never once allowed them to call me God."

I was astounded by her manner of talking as much as what she said. She was, indeed, something of a queen. I could feel her magnetic attraction and why Jakjak remained so devoted to her.

"Tell me Sanfia, zombies are depicted as super-strong beings and tough warriors."

"So they are, but they are more enduring than strong. Their muscles, while wasting from insufficient diets, lack the enzymes and lactic acid that weaken them from prolonged activity. Their muscles never fatigue and they can fight indefinitely, while someone such as yourself, has strong muscles that tire very quickly. Their bones are rigid, like steel plates. With the low demand for blood, the bone marrow that makes the red blood cells is replaced by calcium. They become strong so that it takes more to break their bones than it would to break yours.

"Of course, in all combat, there is a mental quotient. You think you are strong, and that belief will persist in the first of a combat situation, but my zombies have no emotion. When they hear a command to fight or kill, there is no psychological overlay from a conscious mind that detracts or stops them short of a victory. And further, if you shoot them or cut them, even in their vital organs, their blood is thick and the walls of their vessels collapse quickly. Unlike you, when Farok struck your neck and blood flowed profusely even with a minor cut, when they bleed, it is quite slowly. They can survive with an infinitesimally small volume of blood. Their brains and vital organs are accustomed to low blood flow and will live with only a trace of the blood it takes for your body to function. In a battle between a zombie and human, put your wager on the zombie."

Her words and educated manner of speaking were intriguing, but I needed to learn what Farok was planning. "He has alluded to using zombies as suicide bombers, and I can see how their cooperative nature would make them good for this. Tell me, how can he make his own zombies?"

She began to cry again.

Jakjak hugged her tightly.

"It was my fault. I refuse to give my zombie potions to anyone else. Omar tried to create zombies of his own, but they were too 'green,' not the color, but insufficiently drugged, to make them good. So, I taught him to use the zombie cucumber as I had been doing for years on the greenies. But he was impatient as to the length of time it took to make new zombies. Unfortunately, he learned that completely normal individuals become zombies when loaded up with the cucumbers. He has been giving the zombie cucumbers to all the Syrians without the other drugs I normally use to soften the effects. Within twenty-four hours of consuming a diet loaded with the cucumbers, they're like my own creations."

"Why don't *you* do that, rather than the lengthy, detailed process all yours go through?"

"Because each cucumber varies in the amount of medicine it produces. If you load a person up with it, they sometimes die from overdose. They are good zombies up to the time they die, but I don't want any of my children to die."

I nodded. She loved all her "children."

"But Omar Farok cares nothing about them dying. At least a dozen have already died under him and his crude methods."

"How does he administer the drug?"

"All their food is cooked with the cucumber. Using recipes from Syria, like the food you were just served. These people were all hungry when they came here. They eat everything they are given, even though it tastes bad."

"Then, there was cucumber in the food and Arak he tried to give us."

"Yes."

I was curious about the plant she called the zombie cucumber. I was surprised when she took a piece of a green plant from her purse and showed it to me.

I immediately recognized the prickly leaves and the seed pod with sharp spurs. "This is a weed that I had to hoe out of my gardens when I was growing up. Dad called it 'loco weed.' He said it would kill our cows."

"Yes, it goes by the scientific name Datura Stramonium. Jimson's weed is what they call it in America because it was discovered in the 1607 Jamestown settlement."

I held up the plant she gave me. "Where did you get this? From America?"

"No, I have cultivated the plant here on Ile-à-Vache for over twenty years. This is a big farming area. Most of the island's commerce comes from farming. I maintain a ten acre farm for just that. The plant contains medicines you as a surgeon have used in your operations, atropine and scopolamine."

"Yes, we used to use scopolamine in surgery because of it's amnesic properties, but other drugs have replaced it. I use atropine when the heart rate slows during surgery. It speeds the heart up so quickly that I have to give it slowly. Too much kills."

"Yes, yes. It kills if you use too much. When given in large doses, it makes one forgetful. They don't remember anything and they become submissive to any suggestion.

That is what Omar wants. He wants all of the Syrians to have amnesia."

"Like zombies," Jakjak said.

"These people have been here only two days and all are zombies. Now his hotel is scheduled to receive international guests in four days."

"His hotel?"

"Yes. He says he's the owner. The Commerce Secretary wanted to develop this island for the tourist money. Haiti gave him this land for building the tourist resort, such as he's done. His crews have worked around the clock the past six months and completed it three weeks ago."

"But, what happens to all your people, and the Syrians?"

She shook her head. "I don't know. But with the zombie cucumber, he doesn't need to keep zombies as I do. He uses them on suicide missions, then makes more when the occasion rises."

"I need to learn from you the nature of the zombie drugs you used on me and Keyes."

"Do you plan to make zombies as well?"

"No, but whatever you smeared on Keyes' and my heads after Emmanuel smacked us with rocks gave us immunity to Ebola. Farok spread Ebola all over the hospital where I worked, just three days ago. Hundreds of people could die from Ebola if I can't acquire whatever it was that you put in the zombie potion."

"Oh, my," Sanfia said. "I'm afraid I can't help you."

Chapter 29

Sub-basement Jail
12:30 p.m.

"THERE WAS ONLY ONE batch of mixture that had blood from Omar in it."

Sanfia began to explain that Omar had supplied her with the cadaveric material she mixed with the tetrodotoxin from puffer fish and bufotoxin from giant toads. I listened as she told me her exact formula. It was logical that the material supplied by Farok was from exposed beings and that that was the material that conveyed immunity. Sanfia said she only gave the material she got from Farok to me and Keyes. "The blood I used in preparing the zombie potion I gave you came from dead gorillas. Omar gave it to me. Farok thought he could give you Ebola. In fact, he thought for sure that you would die. When he heard you didn't even get sick, he realized he'd miscalculated. He'd made you immune instead. He flew into a crazy rage. He said he would get his revenge on you one way or another."

I thought for a moment, then pointed out: "The gorillas are one of the reasons airborne infections were discredited. They live in the heart of the regions where Ebola has started, but the fact that gorillas haven't got the active disease during epidemics has been a cornerstone of the theory against airborne spread. Regardless, Ebola probably started with primates, long before humans were infected, so maybe, just maybe, a large segment of the ape population is already immune."

I was disappointed. Keyes and I wouldn't be enough to produce the quantity of serum needed to deal with a large outbreak of the disease.

"So we're the only ones."

"Yes, Dr. James. I'm afraid so."

We began to hear muffled sounds coming from what seemed like the other rooms. Angry voices of the Haitian zombies screamed, but we could barely hear them. Sanfia jumped up and shrieked, "Those are my children! My babies!"

She went to the door and screamed, much louder than I thought her capable. "*Pa batay! Fè zanmi ak sa yo, ou frè ak sè!* Don't fight! Be calm, my children!"

The muffled shouting continued and Sanfia screamed out again, with no result. "But they always do what I say."

"They can't hear you," I said. "We can barely hear them."

She nodded, then sat down, defeated.

Jakjak and I searched the rooms for any tools or structural weaknesses that might permit our escape. Farok knew our ability to exploit even small lapses in protocol, and left nothing to chance. My only hope was that the GPS signal had been seen.

Chapter 30

General Perkins' Office
Homestead Air Base
1:10 p.m.

GENERAL PERKINS TURNED HIS chair to face the window. He thought about his career. He sure as hell didn't feel like risking it on a cowboy like Scott James, he thought. "Olivia," he called to the other room.

"Yes, sir," was the response of Lt. Moss.

"Get me the Under Secretary of State."

After two minutes his phone rang. "Arthur, I have a minor problem I'd like to vent with you."

"Okay, Roy. Let's hear it."

"You're aware that we've beefed up the security detail for the CDC in Haiti, right?"

"Sure."

Perkins took a deep breath. "I've been in communication with President Longpre. I've informed him, at great length, of the urgency of the CDC's mission there. This is the group that's trying to find some kind of vaccine for Ebola."

"Yes. I'm aware of that. Madam Secretary has communicated with him as well."

"He directed his police to provide protection for the group, but that idiot, Scott James, wandered away from Longpre's police protection and has shown up on a small island off the southwest coast of Haiti."

"This is the guy that the terrorist cell is trying to kill."

"That's him."

"What is this guy's problem?"

"He's ... Well, let's just say that he's been extremely helpful, but he can be a handful sometimes."

"Sounds like an understatement."

"Yes, well, the CDC representative on the ground in Haiti, Dr. Reed, has made a request that the extra security detail fly their helicopters to the island to find the man."

"Ooh ... God, I don't know, Roy. What's your feeling about it?"

"Well, I'm torn between allowing their request and denying it."

"General, I know your situation. You don't want to take the responsibility for a decision that may backfire on you. We all have our future to think about. This one thing could screw up a lot. We don't want a disaster on our hands. I'd lean in favor of passing the decision on to a higher level."

"The Secretary of State?"

"Yes, but before I drop that on her, I need to check her mood. She's still dodging the controversy over Libya. A lot of people are blaming her for that. She's thinking about a run at the White House, but that'll be down the toilet if another such incident occurs. I have other matters to discuss with her, and will 'test the weather,' so to speak, before bringing up any problem in Haiti. I don't want to inflame her by pushing this in her lap prematurely. Give me a little time. I'll get back to you after our conference, around 6:00 p.m."

"Thank you sir, I mean Arthur."

Perkins hung up and asked Lt. Moss to get Dr. Reed on the line.

When the phone rang, he took a deep breath and said in his cheerful voice, "Hey, Andy. Sorry I was a little abrupt with you. I've just spoken with the Secretary of State's office."

"Thank you for calling Madam Grayson. What was her recommendation?"

General Perkins cleared his throat. "She was in a conference, but I spoke with the Undersecretary, Arthur Johnson. He recommends we delay any action until we gain her clearance."

"Hopefully, that will be soon. The clock is moving on the incubation time for the Ebola in North Carolina."

"It may take a couple of hours. I'll get back to you when I talk to her."

"But I need to know right now!"

"A-*hem*. I understand, and in the meantime, keep me posted on your situation there."

Chapter 31

CDC Temporary Headquarters
2:00 p.m.

ANDY REED PUT ON a surgical mask and gloves and dodged under the make-shift partition separating the lab from the temporary Command Headquarters. The workers looked up from their microscopes, centrifuges, and culture tubes.

"Why so glum?"

The lab chief, Dr. Chang, spoke through his mask. "Bartholome's numbers are all wrong. He probably doesn't have immunity."

Reed's shoulders slumped. "Damn. That's not good."

"The IgG titers aren't there. Hell, the man barely has any blood in him to begin with. He's in terrible shape."

"Okay, let's keep him quarantined, at least for another couple of days. And get some fluids in him. And solid food."

"We're trying. But he's not very responsive. Dr. Reed?"

"Yes?"

"Didn't you say that there were dead zombies back at that house?"

"Yes. I guess we could try to get some material from them."

"How long have they been dead?"

Reed shrugged. "Who knows?"

"Well, we're still doing the work, but Bartholome has very concentrated blood, with high hemoglobins as well. If those other people haven't been dead for very long, and they're immune, they could be useful. On the other hand, if they've been dead for a while, I imagine their blood cells are crenated. I doubt that'll be useful."

"Yes, of course. My God," Perkins said, thinking of his options, "We need to get Dr. James back. We need to draw some more blood. Okay, I'll let Wilson at Jackson City Hospital know the news."

Reed went to the Command Post, took off his mask, and sat down. Captain Roberts came in and took a seat. After a moment, Sarge came in and stood quietly with his arms folded. They all understood how the situation was unfolding. The idea of finding a quick fix wasn't looking good, and worse, Dr. James was no longer in contact with anyone. Reed spoke. "I can't wait any longer. Dr. James couldn't have gone to that island by himself. He was kidnapped. I know James' life is in jeopardy, if he isn't already dead."

Quarantine
Jackson City Hospital
2:05 p.m.

THROUGHOUT THE HOSPITAL, ALL was quiet. The quarantined doctors and nurses were resting from the all-nighters that had followed the bombing.

Sam Wilson's phone rang. "This is Dr. Wilson."

"Sam, it's Andy. I'm afraid our zombie is a bust."

"Damn, that's bad."

"His blood work is all negative."

"Well, we have a little good news from here."

"Good, I could use some."

"The three who had fevers were all strep cases."

"That's it?" Reed asked, clearly encouraged by the news.

"Yup. Just sore throats. Or that's the way it looks right now. We're performing the routine Ebola checks on all those in the hospital. There are no other fevers, not even in the post operative group of those injured in the blast. But it's still early."

"Could be the calm before the storm," Reed said.

"Could be. Your lab here identified the Ebola. It's the Zaire type."

"I saw that. They texted me." Reed replied. "The average incubation period for the Zaire type of Ebola is 12.7 days, so we have a little time. If nobody's febrile for a few more days, maybe we'll have enough immune serum so just maybe nobody will get sick."

"You're a dreamer. But we're all set up. Supplies have flooded the hospital, coming from groups around the world, everything from gowns and gloves to sterilizers."

"Any gifts of Ebola drugs or immune serum? If that comes in, we'll use it immediately."

"Not a single offer. We've contacted the San Diego manufacturer of Zmapp, and they have essentially none available, other than that contracted to Ebola labs in Africa. And they refuse to give us any of that 'sacred' supply."

"What is it with these people? Why is everyone so tight about this?"

"Andy, I've called a lot of people about this and I've never seen people so hard to deal with. Most won't even return my phone calls. I guess they think it's not serious unless you actually have an epidemic."

"You're preaching to the converted, Dr. Wilson. This particular disease has a history, at least in the United States, of noncooperation and poor sharing of information. There is one bright spot. Thanks to the European Medicines Agency's recent endorsement of ZMapp, the company has upped their production."

"All I can say, Andy, is that if the trend does follow what happened in Africa, a lot of people will get sick in the next two weeks."

Chapter 32

General Perkins' Office
Homestead Air Base
3:10 p.m.

Lt. Moss put her hand over the phone and said, "General Perkins, Dr. Reed is on the phone. Perkins looked at his watch: Six hours since James disappeared, and three hours since his GPS blipped on Ile a Vache.

Lt. Moss removed her hand and said to Reed, "What's your question?"

"My question is: Has he talked to Secretary Grayson?"

Moss put her hand over the phone and rolled her eyes. Perkins rolled his, too. Letting out a big sigh, she waited for an imaginary count of five, then responded to Reed,

"No sir. She has been in meetings all afternoon and hasn't called him at all."

"But it's urgent that I take one of his helicopters to Ile A Vache to find Dr. James."

This time, Moss did not feign a conversation with her general. "He says 'No.' We mustn't take any action without going through the proper channels. He refuses to grant your request."

"Thank you," Reed said as he hung up.

Lieutenant Moss reached over the nightstand and hung up the phone, then took the glass bottle of oil in her hands and poured more oil on the General's bare chest, then began rubbing deeply.

"Thanks, Olivia, for taking charge of that matter. Now it's Reed's fault if it all goes to shit. You have matured nicely since coming under my command. I'll remember this when I do your next efficiency report."

Lt. Moss lowered her bra and rubbed her breasts against the General's face. "I don't know how you are so strong all the time, taking on so many other people's problems and doing them all so well. I'm learning so much from you, General Perkins, sir. When I get my command, I want to be just like you."

Chapter 33

CDC Temporary Headquarters
4:00 p.m.

REED, NOW PANICKED A little, dialed the office of the Secretary of State and identified himself. After a few minutes of explanation, he was transferred to the Under Secretary.

"This is Arthur Johnson. Madame Secretary has been made aware of your problem, and she sees this as a matter of utmost urgency and importance. We feel it demands very careful and precise diplomatic negotiations between our two nations. I will be in Haiti on Monday to hammer out an accord. I'll be in touch."

Reed yelled into the phone before Wilson hung up. "Monday is forty-eight hours away! We need authorization NOW!"

Johnson spoke again. "Time is an irrelevant factor, considering the long history of our very delicate relationship with Haiti. When we make our decision, I assure you, it will be in the best interest of all involved."

Reed looked at the phone for a second before slamming it down. He turned to Roberts. "I hear by my intelligence sources that you can fly a helicopter."

"Yes. I'm actually quite proficient at that."

"Captain Roberts, I'd like to take a helicopter to Ile a Vache." Reed looked down for a moment, then looked up at Roberts. "Some people may not like it. I know you probably have a 'promising career' in the Army."

"I'm a reservist. I'm scheduled to be discharged next March. Let'em give me hell 'til then. They can kiss my ass. This is more important. Besides, my instructions are to fly you around. I was told that it was based on your need." He looked at Sarge, "We're going to go run an errand, quickly."

Sarge smiled. "Saddle up and ride."

Chapter 34

Caribbean Sea
5:30 p.m.

REED SAT LOOKING OUT the helicopter window, watching the palm tree-lined coast speed past. Sarge sat opposite him, looking out the other side at the open sea. The sun was setting, which made the Caribbean water a solid blue, without any glimmer of waves. The cockpit seemed strangely empty with just Roberts flying by himself in one seat, and with no copilot in the other.

They'd taken off from the compound very sharply, rising and accelerating forward so fast that Reed's stomach had dropped a bit. Once Roberts had cleared the rooftops he'd made a hard right turn and had flown at low altitude, cross country. Once the south coast was in view, he made another hard right turn and dropped down to wave-top level. It was clear that Roberts was trying to be as hard to see on radar as possible.

The terrain of Ile a Vache was a patchwork. In some places there was dense tropical forest, usually consisting of palm trees surrounded be considerable undergrowth. But there were also plenty of open fields, level and perfect for landing.

Roberts circled over the Grand Beach Hotel twice, then landed the chopper in a clearing, two hundred meters from the resort's grounds.

"We'll be right back!" Reed shouted to Roberts over the engine noise.

Roberts responded by patting his helmet with his hand and mouthing 'call me'."

Reed and Sarge got out, carrying their radios, and started toward the hotel. They walked, hunched over, through thick underbrush, then broke out and walked through the front gate of the resort. They passed magnificent, multi-colored hibiscus gardens, a cement pond with lighted cascades of spraying water, and a rock patio with a twenty foot statue of President Longpre. The place seemed completely normal in appearance and open for business. They passed through the revolving doors of the front entrance and looked up to see the eight floors of silver steel panels paralleling the sparkling glass facade of the hotel. "High dollar," Sarge said.

Inside, they were greeted by a red-suited, black-satin-collared doorman, with a red, silk, top hat. "Gentlemen, welcome to the Grand Beach Hotel. Your host awaits you."

He marched stiffly ahead with a rigid posture, swinging his straightened arms like a toy soldier. Reed and Sarge followed as he led them through an empty lobby to a gold colored door with a crystal knob.

They were led into a large office. Vertical mahogany panels went from the ceiling to the floor, and were adorned with cut glass mirrors. Exotic orchids grew in crystal shelves, projecting from the walls. Three crystal chandeliers hung from the twelve foot ceiling, flooding the room with light.

A man, dressed in a white tuxedo with a high white collar, sans tie, sat behind an enormous desk, looking like a dictator.

Farok stood and bowed. "It is my pleasure to greet a scientist of your stature, Dr. Reed. I am the Great Emir, Omar Farok."

Two guards entered from behind Reed and Sarge and put pistols to their heads.

"I am aware of all the honors accorded you by the medical profession world wide. You will be surprised to know that I support science and have my own brilliant researchers that have worked on projects vital to my inevitable rise someday to ISIS supremacy."

The guards patted down the two men and stripped them of their radios.

Reed asked, "Just what are your 'vital' projects?"

Farok's heels clicked on the marble floors as he walked around the desk to Reed. "My scientists do not possess the lengthy list of credentials that you do, but I assure you, they share your brilliance. Today, my plan is to introduce you to my scientists."

Farok looked at Sarge, "I was curious as to why your pilot didn't have his transponder on." He looked back at Reed. "It is most unfortunate that you have gotten the US Army involved."

"I know Scott James is here in this hotel. I demand to see him."

"Dr. Reed, *tsk tsk tsk,* you're in no position to demand anything. Dr. James has already asked for a tour of my laboratory, but I told him that I would await your arrival."

Farok frowned and clapped his hands. A big fat man dressed in the same colorful uniform as the hotel employees popped in and stood at attention. "Get Dr. James and his black colleague and have them meet us in front of my lab. Bring extra guards, and the stun guns I bought just to control the likes of him. And release the zombies. Tell them to kill the pilot of the helicopter."

Chapter 35

Helicopter Landing Zone
6:30 p.m.

ROBERTS SAT, WAITING, WITH the rotors still turning. He knew his aircraft would attract attention. In the darkness, he could make out a throng of people emerging from a hedge row and walking silently toward him.

More people appeared on the other side of the helicopter. They were all marching slowly toward him. He saw no weapons. Their light, tropical clothing betrayed no rifles or bombs of any kind.

The throng kept moving, showing no fear of the spinning rotors. Roberts looked at a scene he was unable to comprehend. As they got closer, he could make out their faces a little. They all seemed to be blank, as though they were asleep.

Roberts waved his arms, signaling for them to get back, but they didn't seem to be aware of their surroundings. They reached the chopper and started trying to open the doors. Roberts shouted, "Get back! NO! Get back!"

But there was no response of any kind. Half a dozen people were clawing at the chopper, trying to figure out how to open the door. It was hopeless. Roberts thought for a moment, then took off, ascending and flying forward. He gained altitude and flew out over the water. *What the hell was that?* he wondered.

Chapter 36

Research Laboratory
7:00 p.m.

JAKJAK AND I WERE blindfolded, then taken down the hallway, escorted through a locked door, into an elevator, and down to what the guard said was Farok's research laboratory. I laughed when he told me that, but as I walked into the ante room of the lab and had my blindfold removed, I looked through the glass partition at a huge space, half as big as a football field. The main lab was sectioned into at least a dozen smaller labs, all with glass walls. Bright lights reflected off what looked like giant, stainless steel centrifuges. There must have been twenty workers, all wearing white Hazmat clothes and gloves. Each was busy with test tubes or looking through microscopes, transferring materials from one beaker to another using pipettes, and smearing culture tubes.

Four, white and chrome cylinders, stood prominently in the center, projecting up four feet above ceramic desks. All had computers at their sides. I recognized them as electron microscopes, but I had never seen more than two of these million dollar instruments in any of the labs where I worked. Also, strangely, I saw many glass and chrome devices, big and small, such as I'd never seen in any medical lab before.

Jakjak and I were now unrestrained, and I knew this was my best opportunity to escape, but suddenly a door opened and in walked Emmanuel, dressed in a Hazmat suit, holding a pistol on Dr. Reed. Behind them came Farok, also wearing a Hazmat suit, carrying his riding crop in his hand. With him was another man, a tall thin fellow in full Hazmat dress, with glasses on inside his helmet. Seeing Emmanuel again made me gasp a little: Emmanuel, Sanfia's loyal assistant. Farok stood beside him and said, proudly, "Yes. He's on my team now. The little voodoo witch didn't pay him enough money. But through my enrichment, he's the proud owner of a new Porsche and cabana in the Dominican Republic. Isn't that right?"

"Yes, Emir."

Farok patted his broad shoulders.

Farok introduced the thin man wearing the glasses as Dr. Lawrence Pasteur.

Pasteur spoke with a distinct French accent. "Yes, before you ask, I am a descendant, not of Louis Pasteur, but one of his cousins. But I have been stimulated all my life by his work and have dedicated my life to continuing as Louis would have done." He gestured to the lab. "This lab is all my own. I've directed it since its inception."

Farok instinctively swatted him on the arm with the riding crop, then caught himself and tried to force a disarming little smile on his lips.

"But unlike Uncle Louis, who enjoyed taking credit for other researchers work, I must thank Emir Farok for financing the entire laboratory."

Farok glared.

Pasteur cleared his throat and continued, "But I consult the Emir all the time. He has good ideas that help me..."

The riding crop rose a little.

"Well, I mean, I am following his every directive."

Pasteur looked down at Farok, who nodded this time.

Reed looked at Farok and asked, "Just what is your object of study?"

"Ebola. You see, Dr. James' associate, Ms. Keyes, made your government aware of my laboratory in Libya. I had to vacate that facility. It was a pity. I had my publicists make sure that the news reports blamed the US Department of Defense for using the lab to start that 2014 Ebola epidemic in Guinea and Sierra Leone. Unfortunately, they were unsuccessful in preventing the media from discrediting Dr. Pasteur." He patted the arm of Dr. Pasteur.

Reed said, "Ebola's my specialty as well. Do you study immunity, susceptibility, or therapy?"

Farok stood on his toes and exchanged whispers with Pasteur, then he looked at Reed. "Neither. I study viral transmission."

"Then, you propagate the virus to show its virility?"

"I propagate it to infect villages of people."

Reed fell back on his heels as his jaw dropped. "Then, you are planning viral warfare?"

Farok smiled. "That is correct, Doctor. It has been effective for me in several areas in Africa, most recently in Sierra Leone. Four thousand died there, but maybe you can help me with this. In each place I infect a population, after a twenty-five percent infection rate, the disease spontaneously abates."

Pasteur leaned down and whispered to Farok.

Farok looked at Reed. "He tells me you are a stickler for academic accuracy. That figure is 23.8 percent."

Reed looked at Farok and screamed, "Are you nuts?!"

Farok scowled and turned to walk out. "Dr. James has already called me a 'nut case' today. I'll take no more insults. I thought you'd want me to share my knowledge with you."

I stepped between the two of them. "Forgive him, Emir."

God, that hurt me to call him "Emir," but I knew the enormity of this man's inflated ego. "Dr. Reed, tell him how sorry you are and how excited we all are to learn of his discoveries."

Reed said, "Yes, I'm very sorry. I'm as bad as the famous Louis Pasteur in copying the work of other scientists. Tell me more and I'll write papers telling of your academic brilliance."

"I doubt that will be possible, Dr. Reed. But we can look at the lab if you like."

"Great Emir," Emmanuel said, "We must go. The Americans will know we're here very soon. Even if we kill the pilot of the helicopter, they will figure out where he's gone and come looking for him."

"In due time, Emmanuel. I'll not be rushed."

Chapter 37

Farok's Laboratory
7:15 p.m.

Farok opened a tightly sealed door, and we walked into the brightly lit laboratory. I grabbed a paper napkin from the nearby eyewash station and put it over my mouth and nose, then gave one to Jakjak.

Farok seemed to find this mildly amusing. He walked to one of the electron microscopes and talked for a long while about it being the best in the world.

Reed, clearly disturbed, asked, "What's your current project?"

"I am experimenting with new ways to spread the virus so the maximum number of people will die."

In one of the cubicles, a worker used a blower that directed a two inch flow of air into a covered cage.

"In this experiment, I've ordered that a spray of para amino benzoic acid, 'PABA,' with ten thousand viruses, be directed to our subjects. So far, your CDC thinks that only direct contact of body fluids from one person to another will spread the Ebola. Dr. Pasteur believes your CDC is at times backward in resisting this concept. My belief, personally, is that if you were to fire infected blood into an open wound, well ... I think that would be very interesting."

We backed away instinctively from the contaminated spray, which made Farok laugh a little.

I spoke quickly, "There were oxygen canisters in the ambulance that exploded in North Carolina. Was that filled with PABA and Ebola virus?"

"No. But the dead bodies were riddled with it. It was just a little experiment of mine, Dr. James, part of toying with your life for my amusement."

Farok glared at Pasteur, telling him with his eyes that he was in charge of the tour. He continued, "I believe that the virus in the proper diluent will improve 'nature's' delivery of death. I've ordered ten of my scientists to create the perfect liquid that will preserve the virus for many days while our bomb is being prepared for detonation."

Reed looked at me with his eyebrows raised. He didn't need to tell me what he was thinking. There had been no proof, in all the recent Ebola epidemics studied, that airborne Ebola viruses infect.

Reed instead asked, "How did you arrive at the use of para amino benzoic acid?"

Farok smiled and crossed his arms over his chest. "Your scientists never put two and two together."

I raised my eyes.

"PABA is a part of the Folic acid vitamin that your scientists have said is responsible for the reduction of congenital defects in children."

He was accurate in this statement. I had taught families in poor areas to use Folic acid as soon as there was a pregnancy, and I'd seen good results.

He continued, "It has many, many other uses, for hair growth, as an anti aging agent ... but, oh, I'm boring you."

I spoke up, "But how did you ever think of that?" Here, I had to lay it on thick to get him to open up. "You must read all the medical literature to pick up on such a small fact as that."

I could see him smile under his visor. "I read on some of your vials of multi-dose injectables that PABA is added as a preservative. If it preserves the medicines you inject in the muscles and veins of people, it must be safe, and if it goes a step farther and preserves the Ebola virus ... "

He waited for a compliment, so I gave it. "That's brilliant. Maybe the CDC experiments with Ebola didn't work because the virus needed the PABA to keep it alive while a person's lungs reacted to it."

He looked really happy. "Yes, yes, Dr. James. Don't you wish this was your idea?"

I could see the scorn of Dr. Reed as I moved to Farok, placed my hands on his shoulders, and said, "That's brilliant!"

Dr. Reed was having deeper scientific thoughts as he said, "What are the subjects of these tests?"

This excited the little man as well. He walked to a Velcro panel and pulled open a six inch view slot and said,

"Look here. The perfect specimen."

Dr. Reed and I looked simultaneously at a female gorilla, nursing her baby and eating a banana.

I was sick. Gorillas are an endangered species. They need to be protected, not used as guinea pigs for experimentation.

Reed looked away.

I kept my smile and said, "That's the perfect subject. Those animals are more like humans than other experimental animals we've used for this."

I was lying and Reed knew it. Gorillas have been studied in the wild, but I knew of no cases where they had been subjected to anything like this. There was no proof that Ebola virus was spread by airborne particles, and this served only to needlessly kill more of these precious animals.

Reed had to control the tone of his voice so as not to piss off Farok. "How many of these experiments have you performed using this species?"

"There are many of these gorillas in Gabon, and I have twenty more alive in this laboratory and another thirty in vats awaiting their post mortem studies."

Dr. Reed cringed, but he was very good on his feet, so to speak. "In vats? Shouldn't you use refrigeration?"

"No. The PABA I use in aerosols is an excellent preservative for my tissues. Dr. Pasteur and I have learned that PABA does no damage at the cellular level, like ice crystals do in a freezer."

Reed looked like he was about to faint at the more than fifty gorillas used in this totally unnecessary experiment.

Again, I tried to look excited. I shook first Farok's hand, then that of Pasteur. "Congratulations. You should be honored with the same awards as Dr. Louis Pasteur received over a hundred years ago."

Farok smiled as I'd never seen him do, but this expression quickly changed to a frown.

"Great Emir," Emmanuel said, "The zombies have returned without the pilot's head. The helicopter has taken off, maybe back to its base. It will only be a matter of time before they return with troops, maybe within hours. We must leave this place."

Farok faked a yawn. "We'll see."

Chapter 38

Airport
Les Cayes, Haiti
7:40 p.m.

ROBERTS HAD FLOWN OVER the water for about ten minutes before landing at the relatively quiet airport at Les Cayes, on the mainland. He sat in the dark with the rotors turning, waiting to hear from Sarge. He'd called repeatedly on the frequency, with no response. Clearly, something was wrong. Reed and Sarge had been gone too long, and Roberts was starting to feel very strongly that the people who had attacked the helicopter were related to Reed's belief that Dr. James had been kidnapped.

He couldn't circle the island forever, staying in the air, burning fuel. He knew this. But what else could he do? Perhaps the time had come to call in reinforcements, or perhaps his superior officer. He cringed. He was in a gray area. And even though this was Haiti, it would still be very hard to explain convincingly that he couldn't help but feel that he'd just been surrounded by ... well ... *zombies*.

Roberts took off, headed back to Ile a Vache. He flew the seven or so miles over the water, then flew a series of very low passes over the hotel. Maybe if he shook their cage down there they'd show themselves, whoever *they* were. After the third pass at low altitude, he decided to land. There was just enough room in courtyard.

Roberts started easing the bird down. Below him, the trees went wild, as did the plants. He was coming down, for better or for worse. Men started pouring out of the hotel. In the bright lights of the hotel's main entrance, he could see they were armed. One took aim, and fired. Roberts heard the round hit the helicopter. Too hot. He rose out of the courtyard just as a hail of gunfire filled the night air. All of them were shooting at him now, and then he heard the sounds of bombs going off.

Chapter 39

The Sub-basement
Grand Beach Hotel
7:40 p.m.

EMMANUEL AND FOUR OF his Taser-armed guards led us to our cells. He unlocked the door and we immediately saw Sarge, resting on the mattress, and Sanfia sitting by herself, looking defeated.

After they'd left, Reed asked, "What happens now?"

"We've got to figure out a way to get out of here."

Reed turned to Sanfia and said, "My name is Dr. Andy Reed. I work for the Center For Disease Control in the United States."

The decrepit woman said in a tiny voice, "Yes, I know who you are. I'm sorry, but he is the only one." She pointed at me. "Him and the woman. They are the only ones I gave the blood to."

The next sound was a thunderous rumble that shook the building. We heard a creaking of steel first, and then two loud explosions echoed through the halls, followed by a dull *thud* and then a second *thud*. The lights flickered. A deathly silence followed.

Reed looked at me. "Is that an earthquake?"

My stomach rolled. I had an uneasy feeling that the bombs had just detonated and entombed us in this concrete vault forever.

I turned to Jakjak. "We must escape. I'll listen to any options."

Reed said, "When I don't call Roberts or the lab, that will alert them. But how are they supposed to find us? We have to get you back to the quarantine and draw more blood. If that's even possible now."

"Farok probably constructed all this just for us," I said.

Jakjak held his head in his hands. "But Farok says he's gonna have his people cut off our heads."

I looked at him. "You have to remember, Farok makes lots of promises he doesn't keep. He always promises to do things he never had any intention of doing. He does things in a non-linear way. That's one of the reasons he stays ahead of everybody."

I looked at Sanfia. "Do you have any ways of telling anybody on the outside we're here, and to send help?"

"Are you referring to my powers of clairvoyance? You know yourself that is a mental process and renders no magical power."

I looked down. "I know. I'm just looking into my options. We could use some help, even from witchcraft or wizardry."

Jakjak laughed. "Now, doan you go soft on us."

Sanfia stared into space for a second. "My zombies are very strong. If I could talk to them, they'd do anything I asked."

"Like, break down these doors?"

"Exactly. One or two of them couldn't do it, but they have thirty or forty of my men in two of the cells down here. They'll work together and do it, if I tell them."

That made sense to me. "But our problem is that through these thick walls, they can't hear your commands. A good idea, but not in the realm of possibility."

Suddenly there came a voice that sounded like Omar Farok. "Well, my friends, I have buried all of you."

There was speaker mounted in the corner of our room, near the ceiling, but Farok's voice could be heard throughout the makeshift prison. "Dr. James, I must run along now. Your army friends have shown up at the most unfortunate time. Thankfully, only a small contingent of my men know about my private dungeon, so even after your army storms the hotel, I'm sure it will still be a long time before they find you. Long enough to see if my experiment back at your little community hospital worked. Who knows? Maybe you'll be in there long enough to starve, or practice cannibalism. The slow, agonizing death and eating of each other's bodies brings back my love for the Donner Pass story and the 1609 Jamestown cannibalizing of the young girl named Jane. Oh, I love that kind of torture. Regardless of such pleasant thoughts, I've lost millions and millions of dollars thanks to you. But I've recently helped my brothers take over the Syrian oil fields, which I assure you, will cover the losses you have caused me."

Sanfia looked at the speaker and screamed. "How can anyone be so cruel? You are truly a devil, and with all my powers as Vodoun Empératrice of Haiti, I curse you! May you rot in Hell."

Farok could not hear her. He continued. "My mission for God is to kill all infidels, of whom Dr. James is at the top of God's list. But perhaps better than killing you, Dr. James, I will enjoy watching you get the blame for all of these events, and those to come in the next week. Well, due to the sudden inconvenience, I must rush off now. Goodbye to all of you."

Chapter 40

The Sub-basement
Grand Beach Hotel
8:00 p.m.

WE STARTED KICKING THE door and throwing our shoulders against it. It seemed hopeless. It may have just been a door, but as we were now finding out, kicking it down wasn't as easy as it looked in movies.

"My zombies are strong," Sanfia said. "They would destroy this obstacle in a few minutes."

"A lot of good that does us now, seeing as how they're in the other rooms."

"If only I could speak to them for one moment," Sanfia said wistfully.

"You're saying there are zombies in this place?" Sarge asked. "In the other rooms?"

"Yes. They are all my children."

"Dr. James," Sarge said, "do you know what I do in the real world?"

"I have no idea."

"I'm an electronic technician."

"Great. That's great."

"There are speakers in every jail cell on this floor. They all gave off acoustical feedback, at differing times, when Farok was talking."

"Yeah, I know what feedback is. A speaker gives a sound which is picked up by the microphone and is re-broadcast."

"That's what I'm talking about, the Larsen effect."

"Yes. I know what you mean, but how do you know that?"

"I could hear it. Trust me. I know what I'm talking about."

"Okay. But how does that help us?"

"The feedback I heard means that one of the speakers is connected to a mic. We can have Sanfia broadcast a message to her zombies."

"Yes, yes!" Sanfia said.

"But what if the mic is in a room down the hall? That will do us no good."

"But if there's one mic open on the line, I can find the XLR cable that goes to that one mic. This speaker is on a circuit that feeds through an amplifier. Every room will have the same wiring. There has to be an XLR cable."

I didn't know what he was talking about, so I just said, "Tell me what to do."

We gathered around Sarge as he pointed to the speaker. "It's been plastered in. I can get on someone's shoulders, chip away the plaster, pull out the two cables, the XLR, which is the mic cable, and the broadcast wire, which goes to all the speakers I heard, and hard wire a mic."

"I'll do it," Jakjak said. He stood in the corner, then beckoned for Sarge to climb up on his back. Sarge climbed on the back of the sturdy Jakjak, reached up to the high ceiling, and swatted the side of the speaker as hard as he could. Plaster flew everywhere.

"Careful, Sarge," I said. "Our life depends on that one speaker. Fuck it up and we're dead."

Sarge pounded on the speaker and slowly it broke free of the wall. "I see two cables!"

He struggled for what seemed like hours to remove the screws and twist off the cable collars, using his fingernail and then his belt buckle as a screw driver and his mouth for a knife and an extra hand. "How are you Jakjak?" I asked, thinking he may need a break.

"I'm good. Stay as long as you like."

We could see that Sarge had now laid bare two sections of wires. After ten minutes of grunting, he succeeded in snugging a wire to the back of the speaker, but just barely. "I have to hold this for it to work."

I squatted down next to Jakjak and looked at the frail Sanfia and said, "Get up there and give orders to your zombies."

I helped her up on my back, which was alarmingly easy because of her almost non-exsistant body weight, and moved her close to the speaker.

The fragile old woman leaned over to the speaker, and spoke, quietly at first.

I listened for the zombies to respond but heard nothing. "I don't hear anything."

I had that funny feeling in my stomach again. This was the only chance of our getting out of here. I stated firmly, "They can't hear you. You're going to have to talk as loud as you can. Do you know what to say to them?"

Sanfia's lower lip shot up. "Shut up! These are my children and I know how to talk to them!"

She cleared her throat and belted out a hypnotic baritone that none of us could believe. "*Mwen renmen ou, pitit mwen yo. Manman bezwen èd ou. Ou dwe...*"

She talked to them for a full minute, but I heard no response from the zombies. "Is it even working?" I asked Sarge.

"Shhh!" was Sanfia's response.

I listened hard, and then I heard what sounded like someone banging on a far away door. The sound was rhythmic, pounding for ten second sounds, then a ten second pause.

"What are they doing?" I asked.

Sanfia slapped my face with her hand. "Silans!" she hissed. She glared at me for a moment, then slowly leaned forward to the speaker. Her next words were more a cooing sound rather than an order: "*Sa ki byen, pitit mwen yo.* Mama loves you."

I bent my head to the door and listened. I heard nothing.

Sanfia folded her arms and made no further effort to talk to the zombies. I felt disappointment. Obviously, Sanfia had given up on them as well.

Then I heard the zombies screaming. It sounded like the sounds of people in Hell. The screaming got louder and louder, increasing in volume, and then there was the loud, chaotic crash of a group of bodies exploding through a door.

Their screaming grew louder and louder and then there was a banging on our door. Sanfia was shouting to them and they were hurling themselves at our door. You could see it giving way.

Sanfia was shouting in a commanding voice: "*Manman renmen ou. Koulye a pouse di jiskaske kraze pòt la*. Mama loves you. Now push harder until the door collapses."

She turned and backed us away from the door and then stood proud, with her arms folded.

I looked to see the door being jarred, and then it moved against the lock. Suddenly the door separated from its hinges and exploded open in front of us. Three zombies fell in with it, crashing to the floor. They quickly got up and mobbed Sanfia. She hugged them, crying.

More and more flooded into the room with us, waiting to receive their hug from Mama. There were so many in such a small space that I couldn't count them.

A zombie army.

I said to Sarge, "That was pretty impressive."

"Wait 'til I make you a mic out of a matchbox. That'll really impress you."

Chapter 41

The Sub-basement
Grand Beach Hotel
8:40 p.m.

I FOUGHT MY WAY through the crowd and out the doorway, then ran to the end of the hall. A massive square slab of cement, captured in an impressive steel frame work, lay in front of the exit. Reed caught up with me, and said, "That thing has to weigh at least ten thousand pounds."

"This is the earthquake we heard." I examined the steel frame work and the precision of the placement of the cement block in the hallway. It was obvious that this wasn't a structural defect. "Farok planned this back while the hotel was under construction. He built some kind of mechanical release so that he could drop this barrier and seal off the entire floor."

"My God, can the zombies move this?"

"No."

We looked around to see Sanfia standing there with the zombies lined up behind her.

"There is no way," she said.

Reed pointed down a second hallway, one that was poorly lit and seemed to still be under construction. "What's down there?"

"I'm not sure. I don't think we ever went down there. Hard to tell. We were blindfolded most of the time."

We set off walking down the corridor. It was substantially longer than the one that contained the cells. We saw no doors and nothing on the walls. A light bulb hung from the ceiling every fifty feet.

After walking for a few minutes, we finally hit the end: Another concrete slab. "There were two explosions. This one was the one that sounded so muffled. He's blocked the two exits."

"*Dokte*! De ees a space here!"

At the side of the steel frame that had once been the track for the falling slab, there was a small opening in the wall. The weight of the falling slab had dislodged the railing from the walls, and there was now a thin gap.

Jakjak crawled through the punctured wall and I followed. We were inside the shaft that the slab had come down when it had been deployed by Farok. But it was too dark to see, and impossible to know how to climb to the top. Jakjak and I quickly climbed out.

"The way out is through the top of this shaft. But I'm not sure how to do it."

Sanfia stepped in front of me. "But you are forgetting my children."

"But they aren't smart enough to know what to do."

Sanfia grabbed my shirt and shook it. "Just watch, young man. I will tell them exactly what to do."

"Tell them to climb to the top and see if there is a way out."

Sanfia turned to the three forlorned-looking men who had followed her down the hall like ducklings. She pointed to the hole and whispered something that I couldn't make out, and without showing any acknowledgment of her words whatsoever, they methodically climbed into the hole and disappeared.

"But they have to have some light in that dark space," I said.

Sanfia tapped my chest with her long bony finger. "My children have no need for light."

Chapter 42

The Sub-basement
Grand Beach Hotel
8:52 p.m.

WE WAITED FOR A few moments, and then we heard the sounds of sheet metal creaking and groaning, being worked back and forth by the zombies. Then a large piece of metal clamored to the bottom of the shaft. Immediately there came a rain of dirt and dirt clods. Then another piece of torn metal fell. Then more dirt. I climbed halfway into the hole and started pulling dirt out by the handfuls and handing it to Jakjak, who pitched it down the hallway.

Then I heard a dull thud and an immense cascade of dirt fell all at once. I shouted, "Cave-in! Look out!"

Jakjak and Reed pulled my body out of the hole just as a huge, concrete block fell into the shaft, followed by two of the falling zombies. I leapt back in the hole and grabbed a man's ankles and yelled back at Reed, "Pull! Pull us out!"

The man's dirt covered body came sliding out of the dirt and into the hallway. Jakjak dove into the hole and grabbed the second man. We heard him yelling, "I have him, *Dokte*! Pull me out!"

They came out and fell hard on the ground. They were covered in dirt, but besides that, they seemed strangely unaffected, immune to the destruction. The tiny Sanfia called into the hole after her remaining zombie, and we heard him acknowledge her in an unintelligible grunting noise.

Inside the shaft, half-buried in the dirt, was a gravestone. What little light that was cast inside the shaft revealed the etching of a person's name in the stone masonry.

Then, clearly, there was moonlight in the shaft. "Yeah!" I shouted through the hole, "We're at the top!"

I could see that the framework would be easy enough to climb, but nevertheless, I worried about how the frail Sanfia would be able to climb the twenty feet to the surface.

Climbing out, I said, "Okay, we can go. Sanfia, we're going to have to help you out. Jakjak, maybe she can ride on your back, and I'll help pull you up.

"No," Sanfia said. "I want to stay with my children. I am going to make sure that I have all of them. Then I will leave. You go. I don't care what happens to me, but I never want to be separated from them again."

"I understand," I said. "Good luck."

She looked at me for a moment, then said, "Destroy that evil man."

We climbed, hand over hand, up the girders, until we reached the top, where the zombie waited to push us up through the hole in the ground.

We emerged, one by one, with dirt and debris all over us, in a typical, decrepit, Haitian cemetery. Three hundred feet away, on the other side of a dense hedge, The Grand Beach Hotel was on fire.

It was clear that they were abandoning ship. Farok had probably already left, as had his henchmen. The underlings left behind were looting the place. Smoke was billowing out and sections of the hotel had gone dark. The main lights of the resort still glowed brilliantly, and I stood and watched as people ran to cars, carrying things they were taking with them as they fled. The whole surreal scene had the feeling of watching a cruise ship on fire on New Year's Eve.

"We've got to get the hell of here," Reed said, in a half-whisper.

"The landing zone is only a hundred or so meters away," Sarge said.

"Let's go, James! Let's go! Let's get out of here!"

I took one last look at the spectacle of Farok's dying hotel and biological weapons lab, and then turned to run.

We followed Sarge through the undergrowth. It was pitch dark under the trees and tropical plants, and we had to feel our way for the last few feet. Then we entered an open field and were relieved to have a little moonlight to see by. But there was no helicopter.

"What happened?" Reed asked Sarge.

"Don't know. Could be anything."

Sarge walked out to the middle of the field to get a better view of sky. "There he is!" he yelled, pointing at a distant, blinking light, slowly circling in the sky.

"Are you sure that's him? How can you know?"

"I'd recognize one of our birds anywhere. That's Captain Roberts."

We grouped in the middle of the field and waved our arms and jumped up and down. I had never felt so small in such a big world. Trying to signal without the use of light or electronics seemed like a farce. A small crescent moon had risen, but it seemed hardly enough to illuminate our group of four men in an unlit, open field.

In The Air
Ile a Vache
9:00 p.m.

IT WAS COMING UP on two hours and fifteen minutes of flying time, total, since leaving the CDC staging area, and Roberts knew that he would either have to return to the mainland, or put the bird down on Cow Island, permanently. He'd done everything he could to conserve fuel, but now it was critical. Even worse, it was clear that the hotel that Reed and Sarge had gone into was on fire.

One more pass, he thought, then I'll land a couple of kilometers away and report that there's a problem.

That was all he could do. He was out of options.

Roberts pointed the aircraft toward the landing zone and descended. As he flew over for his pass he saw people in the center of the field. Were they dancing or signaling?

Were they those freaks he'd seen before? Were they the shooters who fired on him at the hotel?

He hovered over the landing zone and looked down with his night vision goggles. Those people were definitely not the weirdos he'd seen before. Those people hadn't seemed even *capable* of jumping up and down, that much was for sure. Then he clearly made out the silhouette of a man in fatigues, the bulky, baggy outline of a uniformed soldier. Sergeant Manthripagada.

Sarge.

Roberts slowly descended. As soon as the skids hit the grass, Sarge rushed forward and opened the side door. Dr. James got in. "Damn! Am I glad to see you!"

"We have to hurry. I only have enough fuel to make it to Les Cayes."

Chapter 43

Airport
Les Cayes
Midnight

WHILE WE WAITED AT the quiet, darkened airport, Roberts sat up front and listened to the frequency. Sarge sat with us in the back. Reed had told Roberts to call back to the CDC staging area and get the other helicopter out here to pick us up. Reed would talk to Perkins, explain everything, and have the Army handle getting Robert's dry aircraft some fuel.

Roberts gave us updates every once in a while on our incoming transport. After the turmoil of our escape and then the thunderous noise of the helicopter, the silent grounds of the dark airport were incredibly peaceful.

In the dark, I asked Reed, "What about the gorillas?"

"I know. I know. But nobody's going back into that hotel unless they have some firepower and the ability to locate bombs. They're also going to have to go in full Hazmat, completely suited up. We're going to have to get the damned army over here. But all that'll take time, Scott. We're also going to have to get an animal handler in here. Or we'll just have to shoot them all."

My heart sank.

"It may be the only way, Scott."

"I know."

"In the meantime, you have to go back to the States on the first plane we can get. You have to give more blood."

Sarge kept looking at me in the dark. He looked like he wanted to tell me something. But instead he hesitated. Something was on his mind. I didn't know what to say so I broke the silence: "Well, Sarge, you owe me a mic made from a matchbox."

I thought my comment was funny, but he didn't laugh. He looked at Reed for a second. He seemed to be hiding something, which made me nervous.

"Is there something I can help you with, Sarge?"

He started to smile.

"Dr. James, I kind of know about you."

"About a third of the country knows me right about now. I'm accused of some of the most heinous crimes ever committed. Even though I didn't do them."

"You don't remember me. I met you once. I was about thirteen, I think. My parents came to the States when I was nine. We settled in Jackson City. My dad worked in a convenience store for shit money and no insurance. They had my little sister, Layla." He pointed to his upper lip and said, "And she had a cleft. My parents couldn't do anything about it. Then you came along and fixed it for nothing. We moved to Florida about two years after that. My parents still tell stories about you."

"How's your sister's scar?"

"You can barely see it."

"Sorry I didn't recognize you, Sarge. I have to be honest, I can't recall that particular patient. I've done about ten thousand procedures since then."

"That's okay. When we first met, I wasn't sure it was you. I didn't know *what* to think. I called my mom a couple of nights ago. When I told her that I thought it was you, she started crying." He shook my hand firmly. "I'll tell my mom that I got to see you."

CDC Temporary Center
4:00 a.m.

COMING IN, FLYING OVER the Quonset huts, it appeared that the National Police had thinned out, lost interest. Only a few cars remained, not a mob.

We touched down and walked to the Command Center. The team was already packing up the gear. Reed got on the phone to Perkins.

"I want James to come back with me. I want him under my care and supervision. I want him to sleep. He has to sleep, for an entire day. He's been through an ordeal, as we all have, and I have to draw some more blood from him immediately."

"I'll talk to the FBI," Perkins said, sounding haggard. "They have to have the say-so while this thing is still hot."

"But he's not actually charged with anything, is he? They're not going to arrest him, are they?"

"Not so far. The Justice Department is saying that they want him for questioning." Perkins chuckled a little. "But everybody is saying that."

When he got off the phone, he said, "Okay, we're going back. Our place is at the quarantine. You're going to be with me. I think the FBI will meet us at Homestead. I want you to get some rest. Perkins is going to arrange everything. But something ... Something's going on. Perkins seemed really distracted. He's usually pretty sharp."

Chapter 44

Day 5
Quarantine
Jackson City Hospital
8:40 p.m.

THE PHONE RANG IN the lab. Wilson knew that it was probably *the* dreaded phone call. He knew that it would be coming from the High Probability Ward. Wilson picked up. It was Eileen, the Chief of Nursing. The High Probability Ward consisted of six, sequestered patients. These were the injured who'd been nearest the blast. Just thirty-six hours ago, the ELISA tests on three of the six in that section had showed their titers at zero. Now they were going up fast.

The nurse's voice was quiet and calm, but concerned. "We have a problem. Four have fevers. Two with temperatures of 102 degrees, two with temps of 100.5. The two with the high temps have nausea, vomiting, diarrhea, and redness of the eyes."

"Okay," Wilson said, trying to ignore the wave of dread that had just washed over him. "That's the real deal. Make sure everybody knows you're no longer High Probability. Change your designation to 'Ebola Ward.' I'll be there in a few minutes."

Chapter 45

Day 6
Temporary CDC Headquarters
Jackson City Hospital Parking Lot
11:30 a.m.

KEYES AND I SAT beside each other, having our blood drawn for the second time in less than a week. The CDC trailer contained a variety of rooms, some of which had the ambiance of a modest waiting area in a neighborhood doctor's office. The room we were in was small, but had enough space for four or five people to sit comfortably. There was a TV in the corner, running the news loop, and of course, magazines.

Keyes looked beautiful, even if she looked tired and stressed. I'd filled her in on all the latest, the fact that

Farok could now make his own zombies, that he even had the help of Sanfia's right hand man, Emmanuel, that Farok was now actively engaged in biological weapons research—a thing she already suspected—and about our escape from Farok's hidden prison. "Sanfia wised up," I said. "In a big way. But I don't know what happened to Emmanuel."

We were there in comfortable silence for a few moments, when she looked at me and said, "I love you, Scott. I want you to know that. No matter what happens, I love you. You're a good man."

"Thank you. I'm sorry that we're being essentially kicked out of Jackson City. There's no place here for us now. The Mayor is going to do everything he can to basically banish us."

"We'll find a way to make it, Scott, as long as we stick together."

"Does 'stick together' mean 'get married?'"

"Are you asking?"

"No, not while I'm giving blood."

Keyes burst out laughing. "Well, we'll just have to see, now won't we?"

The television on the wall was set to CNN, and though it was turned down low, we could still hear the news loop. It had been droning on harmlessly while we'd been sitting there, when suddenly, much to our surprise, we saw a familiar face. "Oh my God," Keyes said, "It's Perkins!"

Video of the uniformed general was playing and the newscaster was saying, "Sources are telling CNN that General Roy Perkins, who has recently been the darling of counter-insurgency theory in Washington, is under pressure to answer questions surrounding his relationship with a junior Air Force officer, Lt. Olivia Moss, 24, of Stansfield, Maryland."

There was an Air Force-issue photograph of Moss, looking angular and tanned. "Oh God," I said. "Poor Perkins. He's screwed now."

"I knew there was something going on there!"

The CNN newscaster went on: "According to Pentagon sources, Moss has been on the General's staff for roughly fourteen months. The two reportedly met while jogging, and shortly afterward, Moss, an aspiring writer, began writing Perkins' biography. Sources are telling CNN that Perkins, who holds the title of Deputy Director of National Intelligence, is in hot water over an alleged affair with the young Lieutenant. General Perkins and his staff have been unavailable for comment."

"Oh, Perkins," Keyes said. "Oh, General, you are in so much trouble."

Chapter 46

Temporary CDC Headquarters
Jackson City Hospital Parking Lot
Noon

ANDY REED WALKED IN dressed in his lab coat, and carrying a handful of files. Special Agent Hopkins followed him into the room, looking very cold. "So far," Reed said, "our Ebola epidemic consists of six infected individuals.

"Dr. Wilson and I have worked the phones for nearly a week now, shaming people into being reasonable. We've gained special FDA approval to use Zmapp, borrowing the drug from all sources throughout the world where it had been issued for experimental trials. All of the high probables here have received the drug within five days of exposure.

"All those we've treated have received serum, the 400 cc regimen, except for the first one to become ill. We've given him twice the amount as all the others.

"Between the serum we can make from you guys, and the ZMapp and other stuff, we can probably handle about twenty-to-thirty patients. With this new blood, it even allows us to use the larger measure of serum, 400 cc's.

"It has been six days. There are roughly six-to-seven days left in the average Ebola incubation period."

"But you've got no fevers besides the six who were near the blast," I said.

"No. Frankly everything looks pretty good. But again, it's still early in the game. I won't start dancing in the streets for another couple of weeks."

"If we come out of this with only six Ebola cases, I'll dance with you."

"It's a deal. All in all, it's looking a lot better than it did a few days ago."

"Regardless of the outcome, Andy, you've done a good job."

He smiled, "So have you, Scott."

As he was talking, an image of an airliner appeared on the TV. Keyes shouted, "Farok's plane! Farok's plane! It's Farok's plane! Shhhh! Hold on! Hold on! I want to hear this!"

"…last week after leaving Turkey, met with mechanical problems and was forced to land in Morocco. The Government of Kazakhstan has said that it cannot accept any more Syrian refugees. European authorities have echoed this sentiment, saying that, 'In light of recent

attacks, we are reviewing our policy on taking refugees.'
State Department officials, along with authorities at the
Department of Immigration and Naturalization, have
released a joint statement, saying that, 'We welcome these
families who are fleeing tyranny.' and 'The American
people can rest assured that all the proper security
precautions have been taken.'

"The 'plane without a country,' as it's being called,
will be landing this evening in Virginia. Democratic
Governor, Pace Wilson, has received sufficient votes from
his legislature to accept fifty refugees in his state.

"The President has announced that he will, indeed,
be in attendance. From the airport, the President and other
officials will be going with the refugees by motorcade
to Colonial Williamsburg for a special candle-lighting
service.

"The controversial acceptance of the unwanted
refugees has met with harsh criticism from Republican
Governors. A majority of Republican Governors have
rejected the President's search for places to relocate the
refugees. Some in Washington have accused the governors
of not only a fear of ISIS infiltrators but a fear of the
Muslim faith itself."

"Scott! The President will be there! Scott! Oh my
God!"

I tore the needle out of my arm, slinging blood all
around. I was already dialing General Perkins.

No answer.

"Scott! Farok's going to do something! He'll try to kill
the President!"

"God damn it, Perkins! Pick up! PICK UP!"

Agent Hopkins stepped in front of Reed. "Okay, now what's going on here? What are you doing?"

"Call his office in Washington!" Keyes said.

After two rings, the nasally voice answered, "Deputy Director's Office. How can I direct your call?"

"This is Scott James. I have to talk to Perkins. Right away."

The nasally voice said, "Oh … Dr. James. Yes, well, the General isn't taking any calls right now."

"I have to talk to him right now! It's a matter of national security!"

"The General is indisposed right now. I'll give him your message, Dr. James."

"But—"

"I'll have him call you, okay? He'll call you. Bye bye."

I put the phone to my side. I couldn't believe it. Reed and Hopkins looked at me in silence.

Then the phone rang. It was Perkins. The relief was immense.

"General, the plane coming in tonight with the refugees—it's Farok's plane. He said specifically that he was going to 'kill your highest leaders,' and that means the President and whoever else is meeting that plane."

"No. No. No. Don't start with the conspiracy theories, James," Perkins said. He sounded completely different from his normal self. He sounded like a defeated man. "We've checked out that plane. It's a Kazakh West airliner. The Kazakhstan Government refused them at the last second, so they were going to try to go to Europe. The Europeans don't want them, so we took them. It's good for our image."

"But something's not right, I assure you. The plane disappeared completely for seven days. That's got to mean something."

"No way. That plane landed in Morocco after a mechanical. It didn't disappear at all. They landed way out in the desert, at an undisclosed airport. We talked to their people and they simply kept it under wraps to keep it from looking like the Moroccan Government was accepting them and then kicking them out. And we've vetted them to death. These people aren't terrorists, James, they even have an American escorting them."

"General! You don't know what you're dealing with here! Farok could give those people amnesia. He could manipulate them into doing his bidding. He could do virtually anything he wants if he gets the zombie poisons in them. He is going to kill the President! Don't you understand?"

"Dr. James, do you know how often we hear that the President's life is in danger?"

"But you take those threats seriously, don't you?"

"Yes, of course we do. Not us, but the FBI. But this is pretty thin. And don't start that zombie talk. It scares people. Besides, the Williamsburg event is going to be an extremely closed, controlled event. They've got the Secret Service people all over it."

"I need to go out there. I have to be there."

"What the hell good is that going to do?"

"You said yourself: I'm the only link to Farok—me and Keyes, that is. I can help. If something's going on, I may be able to tell the security people. I know what

Farok's men look like. And Keyes—Keyes knows his whole operation. We have to go out there."

"Dr. James, I'm in a very … uh … compromising position right now. I'm also not in charge of you in the States. Not exactly. That's mainly an FBI operation."

"Then talk to the FBI."

I quickly handed over the phone to Hopkins. I put on my most earnest face. "The General needs to talk to you."

"Hopkins"

Special Agent Hopkins listened quietly for a moment, then said "Yes" and "No" several times, then said, "Okay, do you need to talk to Dr. James? … Oh, okay … Uh … Bye."

She looked at me for a brief moment, then Reed spoke up, "Special Agent Hopkins, forty-eight hours ago I was taken prisoner by a terrorist. I had time to talk to him. I've had time to get to know Dr. James. I can tell you unequivocally that this man is doing everything he can to stop Omar Farok. If he says he thinks that there may be a problem, I'd believe him."

"Excuse me," she said. "Let me make a few phone calls." And then she walked out.

After she'd left, I turned to Reed and said, "Do you have a car?"

"Well, I have a rental that was given to me by the CDC."

"I have to go to Williamsburg. Right now. It's three hours away, if I do eighty all the way. If I leave this minute, I'll just barely make it."

"I don't know, Scott. The last time you bugged out I ended up almost getting killed."

We both laughed a little, though it wasn't really funny.

"How are you going to get past the Secret Service once you get there?"

"I'll have to figure that along the way, but I know one thing: I can't sit here and watch Farok try to kill the President."

Special Agent Hopkins walked in, looking a little harried. "Okay, we're going. I've talked to the Secret Service people as well as my boss. We can go, but only as observers. You can't interfere with the events in Williamsburg. You'll stay with me. If we see something, or I should say, if *you* see something, we'll advise The President's security people."

"Let's go. We have to go right now."

"Just take it easy. We've got a helicopter coming."

Chapter 47

CDC Temporary Center
1:30 p.m.

HOPKINS LEFT TO TALK more with her bosses. Reed went with her, after a final handshake.

The door closed and I wasted no time. "I'd like you to get on your laptop, right now, contact Anonymous, and find out what they know."

"Why are you saying that to me?"

I touched her shoulder and said, "You are one of them, are you not?"

She looked at me, then down at her shoes. "Of course not."

"We have to have any piece of intel that can give us an edge. I need you to do what you can to find something. We won't have time to do it when we're in the air or when we get to Williamsburg. You have to do it right now, while they're arranging transport. Also, going through the trailer's WiFi might be wise. If you hack into the CDC network here, you can work from there. That might be a little harder to trace back to you."

"No one can know, Scott, not Jakjak, not Perkins, no one ... "

"I understand. I'll keep Agent Hopkins occupied. Hurry."

I stepped into the hall and walked to the other side of the trailer to keep an eye on Special Agent Hopkins. The helicopter would be at least another forty-five minutes.

I waited, making sure Hopkins didn't barge in on Keyes. After half an hour, Hopkins looked at her texts and said, "Okay, you may want to grab whatever you have. They'll be here in about twenty minutes."

I hoped that it had been long enough for Keyes to get some kind of information, but when I returned to the suite where we'd been giving blood, she said, "Scott, as far as I can tell, everybody's on board. I can't do much in thirty minutes, but I do have one contact I can always go to for this kind of stuff. This person is on the inside at ... you know ... This person is also connected to some other networks. This person is saying there's nothing out there. No signs. No traffic. No reason to think something's coming. They're saying it's completely legit."

"Could we be wrong?"

"Maybe. Maybe that's not Farok's plane."

Chapter 48

Williamsburg, Virginia
4:50 p.m.

THERE WERE VIRGINIA STATE Troopers and plain-clothes security everywhere. The streets surrounding the grounds of Colonial Williamsburg were all blocked, so much so that we had to walk two blocks just to get near the ceremonies. Hopkins had handed us a couple of pairs of binoculars shortly after we'd arrived. We knew this signified that we would not be getting very close at all. We'd probably end up on a roof top.

We walked through the tranquil grounds, past the old brown buildings of historic Williamsburg. There was an amazing peace to the place, or so I was thinking, when Keyes whispered, "Scott," and took my arm and turned me around. "Look up there."

I looked to the roof of a building on the far side of the grounds: A police sniper.

By the time we got close, the refugees and dignitaries were already at the center of the site, listening to the final remarks of Governor Wilson. We could hear him from the speakers: "Williamsburg Virginia is a symbol of freedom in America, and is the place today I greet these freedom seeking refugees ... "

At the Old Capitol Building, we were quickly ushered in and were taken immediately to the old wooden stairs leading up to the balcony. We could hear the Governor's words, echoing as we climbed the rustic steps inside. " ... who fled their country in search of a free society, a place that welcomes people of all races, all nationalities, and all faiths, to escape the brutality of war, and to work, to worship, and live in peace."

At the top, there were double doors that opened out to a small balcony. The balcony overlooked the grounds and was enclosed by an ornate iron railing.

A police sniper was sitting just inside the open doors, just inside the shadow.

Chapter 49

Williamsburg, Virginia
5:00 p.m.

OUR SNIPER USED HIS rifle's scope to scan the crowd. I looked at my watch: 5:00. I was sweating.

For what seemed like a very long time, we watched the fifty refugees and hospitable citizens of Williamsburg mill around on a relaxed tour of the Duke of Gloucester Street. There were lots of photo ops and selfies, and despite the language barrier, there were smiles and everyone seemed to be genuinely enjoying themselves.

I looked for suspicious faces, for signs of baggy clothes that concealed bombs, gun bulges, Jihadist tattoos, and saw nothing.

I felt strange, like it was all staged, the whole thing, the refugees, the government officials ...

"It's Emmanuel!" Keyes said. "Oh shit! It's Emmanuel!"

"What?"

"Scott, it's Emmanuel! There! Down there!"

I pointed my binoculars at the area below and looked at every face for a moment, then noticed a man much larger than those around him. "Emmanuel! Shoot that guy! Shoot the black guy! The guy in the middle! Shoot him!"

"What? No! I can't just shoot someone!"

Hopkins peered out the door, "What guy?"

"Oh my God, Scott! I think he's wearing a vest under his jacket!"

"Shoot that guy!"

"I can't! I don't know who this guy is."

"He's a terrorist!"

The sniper started talking into his headset.

"Oh my God, Scott, he's looking around. He's really suspicious."

"Shoot that guy! Shoot him!"

"I can't!"

I lunged at the sniper, throwing a shoulder into his side, and grabbing the rifle. Keyes jumped on his back and threw her arm around his neck and pulled him down. The rifle broke free and I turned and threw a body block directly into the center of Hopkins' torso. She slapped down hard on her back. I stepped out on the balcony, rested the rifle on the railing, and took aim. I drew a bead, and then for a tiny second I saw Emmanuel. He'd seen the motion in the window and had turned to look. I saw his hand drop to his pocket, and I pulled the trigger.

The shot broke the afternoon calm like lightning striking the ground. I could see in the scope that he'd gone down immediately. The bullet struck in the center of his chest.

The cop flung Keyes off his back and yelled, "Give me that fucking thing!" And then I gagged from Hopkins' arm around my neck, choking me out.

I heard the screaming from the crowd. I heard Keyes gasping for air after her desperate struggle to hold on to the cop. I heard, "Get on the ground! Get on the ground! Get on the ground right now!" I felt another arm come over my back and then I went back hard onto the floor. A huge weight piled on top and then another and then I could barely breathe. "He's a terrorist!" I shouted. "Get back! Tell them to get back! He's got a vest on! Get away!" And then I don't remember anything.

Chapter 50

Williamsburg Police Car
5:45 p.m.

 IT IS A STRANGE thing to watch a group of grown men and women sort out how you're going to be handled, which car they're going to put you in, who's going to guard you, and how they're going to ultimately, methodically, destroy your freedom.

I sat in the back of the car, with the hard steel restraints digging into my wrists. I sat on my handcuffed hands, moving my weight from side to side to prevent crushing one hand or the other.

Keyes had been hauled away to a different car. The last time I saw her, her face was twisted in pain and she was crying long streams of tears.

Emmanuel had not been wearing a bomb vest. No explosives or weapons of any kind were found on him anywhere. Quite the contrary, Emmanuel Johnson's long record as an employee of various relief agencies including, at times, the UN, made him not a terrorist at all, but a "representative." Just as he had been in Haiti, after the earthquake. I had no delusions about Farok claiming responsibility on this one. There wouldn't be a trace anywhere of Emmanuel being part of his operation.

"Mr. Johnson worked for Refugees International, Dr. James, as well as other organizations," the elderly police sergeant said through the lowered window. He bent down to the car, and said quietly to me, "He met with the President and the Governor, privately."

My freedom was gone, what little I'd ever had. But as I said, I am a scapegoat, an outcast, a person "loosely affiliated with ..." and "known to be in association with ..." There are people and powers who are playing games with my life.

Also by Glenn Shepard

The Missile Game
The Zombie Game
The Encryption Game (2016)

75762488R00139

Made in the USA
San Bernardino, CA
04 May 2018